**"I find yo
hurried
married
are—is ridiculous. And I certainly
don't want an affair with you."**

"Really?" he said politely. "I can think of
plenty of words to describe such a marriage,
but *ridiculous* doesn't come to mind. As for
the affair—I thought we'd already had it."

"We spent a few days together," she
corrected, gripped by intolerable anguish.
Yet she had to send him out of her life.
"I'm sorry, but a tropical fling is not
expected to last beyond the tropics. I'll
always be grateful to you for saving my
life, because I suspect that's what you did."

"Stop right there," he advised with an
inflection so deadly it chilled her into
temporary paralysis. "If you're telling me
that you slept with me out of gratitude, I'll
just have to show you that you're wrong."

Royal Weddings

For richer, never poorer—
guaranteed scandal, passion and wealth!

A pregnant princess. A marriage of convenience
for a renegade prince. Two thrilling connected
stories from favorite author Robyn Donald. Both
Princess Lucia Bagaton and Prince Guy of Dacia
are about to discover that *modern* royal marriage
isn't entirely at their command!

This month, enjoy Prince Guy's story:

Lauren marries Guy in a fake ceremony to escape a
war-torn island, and falls in love with him. But the
marriage turns out to be legal—and Guy to
be a prince, who believes Lauren to be another
man's mistress.... Can they reconcile their
misunderstandings and find the path to love?

Robyn Donald

BY ROYAL COMMAND

Royal Weddings

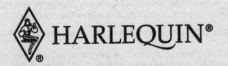

HARLEQUIN®

TORONTO • NEW YORK • LONDON
AMSTERDAM • PARIS • SYDNEY • HAMBURG
STOCKHOLM • ATHENS • TOKYO • MILAN • MADRID
PRAGUE • WARSAW • BUDAPEST • AUCKLAND

ISBN 0-373-12414-7

BY ROYAL COMMAND

First North American Publication 2004.

PROLOGUE

WHEN the hair on the back of Guy Bagaton's neck lifted, he finished cracking a joke with the bartender before straightening to his full, impressive height and allowing his tawny gaze to drift casually across sand as white as talcum powder.

A woman was coming towards the bar, the fierce Pacific sun summoning blue flames from her hair as she emerged from the feathery shade of the coconut palms. Camouflaged by the woven side panels of the bar, Guy admired the way her crimson sarong set off bare white shoulders. On her the all-purpose cover-all looked coolly sophisticated, especially paired with frivolous sandals that emphasised long, elegant legs. Yet he'd be prepared to bet she hadn't come to the resort to lie in the sun; in spite of the sarong and the erotic sway of her hips, she walked with purpose.

Guy's body stirred in primal interest. 'Who is that?' he asked the bartender, pitching his voice so that it wouldn't travel.

The barman looked up. 'That's Ms Lauren Porter—got in on the plane from Atu a couple of hours ago. She's staying two nights.'

'I see,' Guy said without expression.

When the manager had rung Guy an hour previously, disturbed because their newest guest had broached her intention of visiting a mountain village, the name had rung bells somewhere in his mind. It hadn't taken him long to trace the thin thread of memory to its source—

a conversation a few months ago with one of his cousins, an elderly Bavarian princess who had a keen nose for gossip and a connoisseur's eye for a good-looking man.

'I noticed you talking to Marc Corbett and his charming wife,' she said after one of her famous dinner parties. 'I wonder if Paige knows that he keeps an English mistress.'

'I doubt it,' Guy said curtly. Paige Corbett had struck him as straightforward and very much in love with her husband, a magnate with varied interests and a reputation for honest dealing.

'Not many people do; they are very discreet and never seen together, but of course you can't stop gossip—someone always knows. She is a Miss Lauren Porter, who is long-legged and beautiful and English. She works in his business. Very clever, I'm told. She has been close to him for years now.'

Guy raised his brows but said nothing.

The elderly princess nodded. 'And now you don't like him very much. Even as a child you had a rigid sense of honour. I like that in a man—it's so rare.'

He'd smiled cynically down at her, but his respect for Marc Corbett had lessened. When Guy made promises he kept them.

Now, narrowing his eyes against the tropical sun, he watched Lauren Porter approach the bar. Her travel arrangements had been made by the Corbett organisation, so this had to be the same woman.

What the hell was she doing here?

When she got close enough for him to see her face, he blinked in something like shock and inhaled swiftly. An enchantress—no wonder she kept Marc Corbett on a leash! Skin like silk, large eyes so pale a grey they glinted uncannily like crystals, and a mouth sultry enough to set the world aflame, allied to a body that gave new meaning to the words sexual chemistry—Lauren Porter had all the necessary attributes for a mistress.

Why did she plan to visit a small, dirt-poor village in the mountains? It had to be business, and so it had to be connected to Marc Corbett, who had fingers in all sorts of industrial pies around the world.

Ignoring the reckless drumming of lust through his body, he frowned and watched her veer away from the bar and disappear into the reception area. He'd better go and find out what she was up to.

It shouldn't be too difficult to persuade her not to leave the resort; women who looked as though they'd just emerged from a fashion magazine scared easily. He'd mention that mountain cockroaches were huge, follow it up with an allusion to leeches, and she'd probably pass out.

Yet even as he grinned derisively, that sense of unease, of prospective danger, thickened around him. Although he had no information to back it up, the tenuous foreboding had been correct too often to dismiss; a couple of times it had saved his life.

He should have collected his mobile phone from the office before coming down to the resort.

'So you've heard nothing about any problems,' he said to the bartender.

The man shrugged. 'There's talk,' he said, 'but on Sant'Rosa we talk a lot.'

'Sit in the bush and drink grog and gossip,' Guy returned tolerantly. 'OK, forget I asked.'

The young man had been polishing glasses. He

stopped now and looked up, the concern in his dark eyes and dark face mirrored in his tone. 'What have you heard?'

'Nothing,' Guy told him truthfully. 'Not a single thing, but you know me— I like to gossip too.'

'War,' the bartender said wearily, picking up another glass. 'We hoped it had finished, but since this preacher started talking about John Frumm bringing in food and drink and cigarettes and all the good things from America, people are getting nervous.'

'I know. Just keep your eyes and ears open, will you?' Guy nodded towards the reception area. 'I think I'll go and make the acquaintance of Ms Porter.'

And once he'd convinced her a trip into the mountains wasn't feasible, he'd talk to the receptionist. She came from a village close by the border, so she might have heard something that would explain the elemental warning running down his spine like a cold finger.

The younger man grinned. 'That Ms Porter, she's pretty—skinny, though. Don't know why you Europeans like skinny women.' He shook his head over the weird tastes of western men, then added, 'She's nice—she smiles and talks to you when you carry her bags.'

She wasn't smiling when Guy stopped just outside the door to the entry lobby; she was talking so intently she hadn't noticed him arrive.

Recalling a fairy tale his English nanny had read to him, he thought, *Hair black as coal, skin white as snow, lips red as roses...*

Up close, she wasn't beautiful, but with a mouth that fuelled erotic dreams, who cared? His body certainly didn't; it was at full alert.

Yet in spite of that mouth and the high, small breasts

and slim waist beneath the sarong, Lauren Porter was all poised control, even though she wasn't getting what she wanted.

Time to bring on the cockroaches, Guy decided ironically, and stepped inside out of the sun.

CHAPTER ONE

L<small>AUREN</small> frowned. 'Do you mean it's *impossible* to get to this village?'

The receptionist hesitated before saying cautiously, 'It is not impossible, ma'am, but it is difficult.'

'Why?'

Anxious brown eyes avoided Lauren's in a respectful manner. 'The road is too dangerous, ma'am.'

On Sant'Rosa the word road was used loosely; the memory of the minibus juddering violently sent a reminiscent twinge through Lauren's body. And that was on the road from the airport to the resort.

The prospect of tackling an even worse route wasn't pleasant. So what, she thought grimly, was new? Nothing about this side trip had been easy.

Not for the first time, she wished she hadn't promised to check out Paige's favourite charity. In London it had seemed simple, a mere matter of breaking her journey to a New Zealand holiday with a couple of days on a tropical island.

Ha! Her flight to Singapore had been delayed so she'd missed the connection, and as she hadn't got to Sant'Rosa until after midnight she'd had to wait for the early-morning plane to the South Coast.

After only a couple of hours' sleep, her head was aching, her eyes were gritty, and her smile was hurting her lips. And now this! She pushed a stray strand of damp black hair back from her cheek. 'What about public transport?'

Still avoiding her gaze, the receptionist stopped shuffling papers to adjust the scarlet hibiscus behind one ear. 'Ma'am, there is nothing suitable for you.'

'I'm perfectly happy to go on the local bus,' Lauren said crisply.

The woman looked harried. 'It is not suitable,' she repeated. 'And that village is very alone—apart.'

The village had set up an export venture that involved a factory, so it couldn't be too isolated. A steely note running through her words, Lauren persisted, 'In that case, where can I hire a car?'

From behind a hard masculine voice drawled, 'You can't. There are no car-hire firms on the South Coast.'

Lauren stiffened, every sense sounding alarms. The new arrival's voice—deep, subtly infused with irony— oozed male confidence.

Slowly she turned. Although tall, she had to look up to meet half-closed topaz eyes between lashes as dark as her most forbidden desire. Her stomach—normally an obedient organ not given to independent action— lurched, then dropped into free fall.

Inanely she repeated, 'No car-hire firms?'

'Lady, the closest car-hire firm is in the capital, and that, as you already know, is an hour's flight away over a mountain range.'

He infused the word *lady* with a slow, purring sexuality that fanned over her skin like the warm breath of a lover. *And where did that thought come from?* Clutching her tattered dignity around her, she asked crisply, 'Then how can I get to this village?'

Because she couldn't pronounce the name she thrust out the slip of paper Paige had given her.

His expression altered in some subtle way as he examined it, but his tone didn't change. 'I doubt if you can. The last rains brought down half a mountain onto the road.'

'Surely they've fixed it.'

One dark brow—his left, she noticed—lifted in sardonic amusement. 'The locals walk it, and as you may have noticed, Sant'Rosa hasn't yet flung itself headlong into tourism. It's still trying to get over a civil war.'

'I know that.' Someone should tell him that the purpose of designer stubble was to emphasise boldly chiselled features, not blur them. And his black hair needed cutting.

A second glance convinced her that the shadow across his jaws and cheeks wasn't for effect—this man hadn't shaved because he didn't care what people thought of him. From the corner of her eye she catalogued the rest of his assets, admitting reluctantly that the overlong black hair had been well cut, and stubble couldn't hide strong bones and a mouth that combined sculpted beauty with a suggestion of ruthlessness.

An elusive flash of memory teased her brain. Somewhere she had seen him...or someone who looked like him?

Startled, she pinned a brief, dismissive curve to her lips. Of course she didn't recognise him! An unkempt expatriate on an island in the middle of the Pacific Ocean was as far out of her ken as an alien. The men she met as a junior executive wore suits and strove for worldliness. This beachcomber, clad in an old black T-shirt and trousers, looked as though neither the word *sophistication* nor the concept existed for him.

She took a deep breath and spoke clearly and carefully. 'Can I fly in? Ms Musi—' she indicated the receptionist, who was gazing at the newcomer as though he'd saved her from a shark '—tells me that the local public transport isn't suitable.'

'She's right.'

'Why?'

His eyes glinted. 'Would you be happy to travel on the back of an elderly, bullet-holed truck with no shelter from the sun and no seats?'

'If I had to,' she said curtly.

'And cockroaches.' No malice coloured the words as he said, 'Big, black ones. If you go to sleep they chew your toenails.'

Hoping he couldn't see her skin crawl, she snapped, 'I can cope with the local fauna.'

'I doubt it,' he drawled. 'If you're really determined to get there, you could try walking.' He inspected her without haste before adding gravely, 'But if you go like that you'd better invest in some sunscreen.'

Who was this sarcastic newcomer with mocking eyes and far too much presence? The manager? Hardly, but it was typical of this trip into the wilds of the Pacific Ocean that she should be confronted by a scruffy deadbeat with an attitude—and a bewildering, raw sex appeal that set every treacherous nerve in her body jangling into awareness.

Her composure evaporating under the impact of his lazily appreciative smile, Lauren stiffened. All right, so the pretty sarong in her favourite shade of crimson revealed an uncomfortable amount of white skin, but she wasn't an idiot! Forcing her voice into its usual confident tone, she asked, 'How long would that take me?'

'It depends how fast you walk. Don't stop for long or leeches will bite you. Do you know how to take a leech off your skin? Remove the small end first—'

The receptionist broke in. 'Mr Guy is making a joke,

ma'am, because it is too far for you to walk.' She gave him a shocked look, as though this wasn't what she expected from him. 'It takes two days to come by walking, ma'am.'

Mr Guy didn't exactly tell her who this man was, but at least his name gave her a handle.

In a voice that blended satire with long-suffering, he said, 'Your travel agent should have warned you that this region is pretty much without civilisation.' He paused a fraction of a second before finishing, 'As you'd know it, anyway.'

'As you know nothing about me, I'm going to ignore that remark!' Furious with herself for letting him get to her, she reined in her temper.

Fortunately the receptionist burst into the local language and the newcomer turned to listen, obviously understanding every word.

Skimming a cold grey glance over the T-shirt and trousers moulded lovingly to long, powerful legs and lean hips, Lauren was forced to revise her first impression. This was no loser. His thrusting bone structure—high cheekbones and a chin that took on the world—spoke of a total lack of compromise.

And now that he'd dropped the mocking veneer, neither old clothes nor villainous stubble could hide his formidable authority. Beneath the beachcomber persona was pure alpha male, testosterone and arrogance smoking off his bronzed hide like an aura. Untamed, certainly, but—intriguing, if you fancied men who looked as though they could deal with anything up to and including marauding Martians.

In other words, she thought hollowly, just the sort of man to take her to Paige's pet village—if she could ignore the instincts that warned her to run like crazy in the opposite direction.

He looked up, meeting her sideways glance with a coolly speculative survey.

Lauren's self-possession crumbled under an awareness as steamy and ruthless as the tropical heat. Not my type! she thought fiercely. She preferred men with at least basic social skills. More colour stung her skin, fading swiftly at the note of desperation in the receptionist's tone.

Black brows meeting above a nose that hinted at Roman gladiators, the newcomer posed several staccato questions, to which the woman responded with increasing reluctance.

Feeling like an eavesdropper, Lauren examined a rack of postcards. Fans hummed softly overhead, sending waves of sultry air over her bare arms. The small resort promised total relaxation, and what it lacked in modern luxuries it made up for in exquisite beauty and peace. Until this man appeared she hadn't missed airconditioning a bit.

Now, in spite of the heat, she wished she'd slung a shirt over her shoulders before leaving her cabin.

Eventually the receptionist's lengthy explanation—punctuated by worried glances at Lauren—wound down to a conclusion.

Something was clearly amiss; a chilly emptiness congealed beneath Lauren's ribs, but she hadn't come all this way to be fobbed off.

The man turned to inspect her. 'Why do you want to go to this village? It has no accommodation for tourists, nothing to do. The only bathroom is a pool in the river. They are not geared for sightseers.'

He had a faint trace of an accent, so elusive Lauren

wasn't sure it existed. Exasperated by the beads of moisture gathering across her brow and top lip, she evaded his question. 'I know that, but I'm not planning to stay. All I want is to spend an afternoon there. In fact, that's why I came to Sant'Rosa—specifically to go there.'

'Why?'

'I don't see that it's any concern of yours.' Lauren didn't try to hide the frosty undertone to her words.

He shrugged broad shoulders. 'Whatever your reason is, it's not good enough,' he said flatly, and forestalled her instant objection. 'Come and have a drink with me and I'll explain why.'

Was this merely a pick-up? Obscurely disappointed, Lauren glanced at the receptionist, who hurried into speech with an air of relief. 'Mr Guy will help you,' she promised, indicating the man with a wave of one beautiful hand and a smile that paid tribute to his potent male magnetism.

OK, so he wasn't a rapist or serial killer. Not here, anyway.

'In that case, I will have a drink, thank you,' Lauren said calmly, wishing that she'd worn something cool and well-cut and sharply classical—and a lot less revealing.

And it would help to have some make-up to shelter behind; sunscreen and a film of coloured lip gloss were flimsy shields against the hard intimidation of his gaze.

The man beside her walked as silently and easily as a panther, his controlled grace hinting subtly of menace. Lauren resented the way he towered above her, especially as each inch of powerful, honed male exuded a potent sensuality.

So his name was Mr Someone Guy. Or Mr Guy

Someone. And she wasn't going to tell him who she was; if he didn't have the manners to properly introduce himself, she certainly wasn't going to make the effort.

As though he felt her survey, he shafted a glance her way. A high-voltage charge sizzled between them, part antagonism, part heady chemistry. Tension jolted her heart into overcompensation.

Turning her face resolutely towards the small bar, she decided wildly that he was wasted here. A man who gave off enough electricity to melt half the world's ice caps should head for some place where his talents could be really appreciated.

The North Pole, for instance.

Who was he? The local layabout, angling for a wild holiday fling? Or perhaps looking out for a rich, lonely woman to rescue him from all this tropical heat?

No. Disturbingly sexy he might be, but instinct warned her he was more buccaneer than gigolo.

In the voice her half-brother, for whom she worked, referred to as Patient but Friendly Executive, she asked, 'Do you own the resort, Mr Guy?'

Winged black brows lifted. 'No,' he said briefly. 'It belongs to the local tribe.' Without touching her, he steered her across to a table beneath a large thatched umbrella. 'This is probably the coolest spot around, and it's got a good view of the lagoon.'

Grateful for the shade, she lowered herself into a chair and persevered, 'But you live here? In this particular area of Sant'Rosa?' she amended, when his brows lifted in saturnine enquiry.

'Off and on.' He nodded to a waiter. 'What would you like to drink?'

'Papaya and pineapple juice, thank you.'

He ordered it for her, and a beer for himself. A tiny

gecko scuttled across the table; smiling, Lauren watched it disappear over the edge. When she looked up, Guy was watching her.

'You're not afraid of them?' he asked.

A subtle intonation convinced her that he wasn't English. 'Not the little ones, although some of the big ones have a nasty predatory gleam in their eyes.'

He laughed outright at that—another slow, sexy laugh that brushed her taut nerves with velvety insinuation.

'They won't bite, not even in self-defence,' he said, stressing the first word just enough for Lauren to immediately wonder if he bit—and when...

He finished, 'But you'd be surprised at the number of women who are terrified of even the tiny ones.'

'Men too, I'll bet. It makes you wonder why some people come to the tropics.' Was the stubble soft to touch—or bristly? She'd never kissed a man with that much—

Whoa!

He leaned back in the chair, his pose utterly relaxed, but his level, cool gaze held her prisoner. 'So why are you here? More specifically, why are you determined to find your way to one of the more untamed spots on Sant'Rosa?'

She parried, 'Is that untamed as in dangerous?'

'As in without conveniences,' he told her, his keen gaze steady and intimidating. 'But it's in the border area, and the border between Sant'Rosa and the Republic has always been tense.'

'I thought the treaty after the civil war stopped the threat of an invasion by the Republic.'

Wide shoulders lifted in a slight shrug. 'A new player—a charismatic preacher—seems to have got together a ragtag following on both sides of the border. He's preaching part religious revival, part cargo cult. Which is—'

'I know what a cargo cult is,' she said crisply. 'Its followers expect a saviour to bring them the benefits of western civilisation. I'd not realised they could be violent.'

'So far they're not, but over the past couple of days there have been rumours that someone is supplying them with weapons.'

Not that anyone had actually seen the rifles and explosives that were being talked about. Guy suspected they didn't exist. However, every islander was taught to use a machete from a very early age, and he'd seen the damage the long blades could inflict. If—and it was a big if—any hyped-up converts decided to go on the rampage, they could kill.

He watched her slender black brows draw together. What the hell was she doing here? And why was she so evasive? Women like her—sleekly elegant from the shiny top of her black head to the polished nails on her toes—demanded more from their holidays than a tiny resort with little social life and a heavy emphasis on family groups.

She looked up sharply, the eyes that had been ice-clear now silvery and impossible to read. 'Only rumours?'

'Almost certainly. Rumours—most of them false—run hot through Sant'Rosa. The people are barely coping with the aftermath of a bloody ten years of civil war, and in spite of the peace treaty they still don't trust the Republic over the border.' He paused. 'The receptionist comes from the village you want to visit, and she's just told me that the preacher has disappeared.'

'And that's bad?'

'Almost certainly not,' he said, hoping he was right.

Because it was too easy to watch her face, he switched his gaze to a family, parents shepherding two small children. Armed with beach toys and a couple of inflatable rings, the children dashed into the improbably turquoise lagoon, yelling and laughing as they splashed each other and their parents.

That itch at the back of his neck sharpened his senses to primitive alertness, a fierce, feral reaction to stimuli his rational brain couldn't process.

Which was why he was resisting the compulsion to bundle up these helpless family groups—and the woman opposite with her cool touch-me-not air—and get them out of here on the next plane.

He didn't dare follow his impulse because the local tribe had sunk every bit of cash they had into the resort; a false alarm, with the resultant bad publicity, could see them lose it all.

The woman opposite was watching the group too, her mouth curving as one of the children shrieked with delight. Grimly, he cursed his unruly loins for responding to that smile with piercing hunger.

Lauren Porter frowned. 'So are this preacher's followers likely to turn violent when no saviour turns up with all the blessings of western civilisation free for the taking?'

'I doubt it. They've seen what fighting does, so they'll almost certainly drift off through the bush to their native villages.'

But they were edgy and frustrated. Peace hadn't brought the people the benefits they'd longed for, and many were ripe for unscrupulous manipulation. When the promised saviour didn't eventuate the preacher might try to salvage his slipping authority by suggesting they collect the material benefits from the nearest place that had them.

They wouldn't go to the mine, which had its own private security force; they'd choose easy pickings. In other words, the resort.

All ifs and buts, with absolutely nothing to base it on. Guy shrugged, trying to banish that needling premonition.

'But they might not,' she said shrewdly, and echoed his thoughts with uncanny accuracy. 'Perhaps they might decide to come and get the goodies for themselves.'

'It's unlikely, and even if they did, the police are watching the situation very closely. The resort would be notified in time to get you out.'

'And everyone else too, I hope.'

'Trust me,' he said with a smile he hoped was reassuring.

The arrival of the bartender with their drinks silenced her; Guy eyed her from beneath his lashes, controlling the sharp appetite her presence roused. The combination of thoroughbred lines and the gentle curves of her breasts and hips packed an explosive impact. Mix all that with silky black hair and eyes of cool, translucent grey, and you had trouble.

He wasn't even going to think about her mouth; it did serious damage to his objectivity.

Lifting his beer in silent salute, he said, 'At the moment it wouldn't be sensible to go into the mountains.'

'What about you?' she asked abruptly.

'What about me?'

'Would you go there?'

'If I had to,' he said warily, watching her.

'So you could take me with you to the village?'

Even softened by femininity, her jaw was combative. God save him from stubborn women, and this one in particular. 'I'm not taking you there,' he said curtly.

'Of course I'd pay you.'

'Lady,' he said, angry in a way he'd never experienced before, 'I am not going, and neither are you. If you want to see how the third world lives, the resort will organise a tour to the local village.' His voice was scathing.

Colour swept along those high cheekbones and her teeth clamped down on her bottom lip.

Guy resisted the urge to lean forward and put a hand over her mouth to stop the ravaging of that ripe bow. He'd take much better care of it than she did...

It was no better when she drank some of her juice; how the hell did she make a simple act like that signal a prelude to sex?

Get over it! he ordered savagely.

Putting the glass down, she fixed him with a determined gaze. 'I want to visit that particular village and tribe because a—a friend of mine has helped them set up an oil industry from *sali* nuts. I'm on my way to New Zealand on holiday, and I promised my friend I'd see how things were going.'

Marc Corbett, of course. Guy nodded, watching her from beneath drooping lashes. 'Then you'll have to tell *your friend* that I wouldn't let you go.'

He wasn't disappointed by her reaction to this deliberate provocation. Her smile froze, but she let it linger as she reached for her glass and lifted it once more to her mouth, keeping her gaze on his face while she drank the juice slowly and delicately.

Although he knew exactly what she was doing—using her female appeal as a weapon—his pulses jumped, and a carnal urgency heated his blood. When lust hit inconveniently he could usually kill it without too much effort, but this time he had to wrestle it back into its lair.

'Well, that's a moot point,' she said sweetly, putting the glass back down. 'I don't know that you have any authority to stop me.'

She didn't lick the juice from her lips; she wasn't so obvious. Guy counted to ten before saying bluntly, 'I'll stop you if I have to handcuff you to my side until I can put you on a plane out. Going into the mountains might well be dangerous; if you pay enough you'll probably get someone to take you, but you'll be putting them in danger too.'

Her eyes were translucent, the grey soft as a dove's breast, but intelligent and searching. She scrutinised him for several long seconds before nodding. 'Yes, you really do mean it. All right, I won't go.'

Surprised by relief, Guy picked up his beer and took another long swallow, welcoming the cool bitterness before realising that she hadn't actually said she wouldn't try to go. 'Give me your promise that you won't leave the resort.'

She looked at him with stony dignity. 'You have no right to demand any promise from me, but I'm not stupid; I don't want to put anyone in jeopardy and neither would my friend. I wish I could get in touch with the headman, though, just to ask how the scheme is going.'

That he could give her. 'As far as I'm aware, it's doing very well, but if you want to contact him, I have a mobile phone in my office,' he offered.

She sent him a glance, cold as moonlight, from beneath her lashes. 'Thank you, but I'll ring from here,' she said politely.

'You can't.'

When her brows shot up he explained, 'After the civil war each village chief in this area was supplied with a mobile phone. Their link isn't connected to the ordinary telephone system, which doesn't extend much beyond the towns.'

After a moment's pause she said, 'I see.' And added on a sigh, 'It's so beautiful here, like paradise. Why can't it be peaceful too?'

'There's always a serpent,' he told her laconically, getting to his feet. 'And usually what it wants is power and money.'

'Do you think this has anything to do with the fact that there's a huge copper mine in this part of Sant'Rosa—and that the area has been under claim by the Republic for fifty years or so?'

'You've done some research.'

'I always research,' she said calmly, thick lashes hiding her thoughts.

When they flicked up again she gazed at him with a limpid innocence that sent suspicion bristling through him.

He jibed, 'And now you know its limitations.'

She ignored that. 'It seems interesting that the preacher started destabilising the border area just after the international peacekeeping force left. If I were cynical, I might wonder whether the Republic hopes that perhaps they can use the cargo cult to foment trouble, then invade under the excuse of preventing yet another civil war.'

He nodded. 'I'd call that realistic rather than cynical. Especially as the Sant'Rosan army is very small, and made up of units that still don't trust each other after fighting on opposite sides in the war. How they'd fare in battle no one is prepared to say.'

'Do you expect war?'

'No.' He drained his beer and set the bottle down on the table with a sharp clink. 'Come on, we'll go into town.'

'Town?' Lauren asked foolishly.

His brows lifted. 'You wanted to use the telephone, didn't you? It's in my office in town.'

When she didn't immediately answer he added with mocking amusement, 'You'll be perfectly safe with me. I have a reputation to uphold.'

And because she didn't suspect him of anything more than an overdose of testosterone, she shrugged slightly and got up to go with him—although not before stopping at the reception desk to tell the woman where she was going.

That done, she hitched her bag over her shoulder. 'I'd better go and get some money,' she said brightly. And after she'd extracted her money from the safe that held her papers, she'd sling a shirt over her shoulders.

With an amused glance he opened the door for her. 'Why? I don't expect payment, and the shops aren't open so late in the day. Even if they were, I doubt very much whether you would find anything to buy in them.'

Bother. She summoned her most dazzling smile, recklessly glad when she saw his eyes darken. 'You'd be surprised,' she said sweetly, going through the door ahead of him.

CHAPTER TWO

Guy's vehicle could probably take the terrain on Mars in its stride. An elderly Land Rover, it possessed only the most basic conveniences and had never had air-conditioning, but that was all right; it didn't have any windows either.

'At least it doesn't have bullet holes,' Lauren observed with a kind smile that might have been overdone.

'Only because I had them taken out,' he said blandly, opening the passenger door for her. 'It probably has cockroaches, though.'

She gave him a repeat of her smile, and forced herself not to search for insects while she waited for him to get in. Because her father, a motoring enthusiast, had taught her to recognise a well-tuned engine, she was surprised when he switched on the key; the battered, dusty vehicle ran like a dream.

Guy Whoever—or Whoever Guy, she reminded herself scrupulously—was familiar to the locals; most waved cheerfully at him, flashing smiles as he tooted in return.

She turned around to gaze at two small boys, hand in hand on the side of the road. 'Are they born with machetes over their shoulders? They look far too young to be carrying such dangerous implements around with them.'

'They call them bush knives here, and yes, they learn to use them almost as soon as they can walk.'

Rebuffed by his indifferent tone, she concentrated on

admiring the jungle and the range of mountains ahead, purple-blue in the distant haze that indicated the approach of dusk. When they arrived at the little town, some miles along the road to the mine and the airport, the empty streets gave it a disturbing, almost sinister atmosphere.

'Dinner time,' Guy said laconically, stopping outside the only block of shops in the scruffy main street. He cast her an enigmatic glance. 'The women prepare the food while the men wind down.'

Refusing to rise to the bait, she shrugged and opened the door to get out.

'My office is on the first floor.' Guy indicated a flight of stark concrete steps rising from the street.

Noting the casually efficient way he examined the street and the stairs, Lauren decided that he'd know how to deal with any threat. His seamless air of confidence placated fears she hadn't allowed herself to recognise.

A large, anonymous room, his office was at least clean and tidy, with everything locked away in steel cabinets.

'To keep the insects and vermin out,' Guy said when he saw her looking around.

When eventually they got in touch with the headman of the village, Lauren spoke to him for some minutes, straining to follow his heavily accented English. The *sali* nut scheme was coming along well; the chief told her proudly of the oil-extraction process, and the amount sent to be turned into soap and other toiletries in New Zealand, and the teacher who had come to live in the village once they'd built the school.

'I'll tell the person who sent me,' she said. 'I've been told it might not be a good idea to travel to the village just now.'

'Not good, ma'am,' he said somberly. 'There are too many rascals around now. Come back next year, when it is quiet again.'

'If I can,' she promised.

From beside her Guy said, 'I'd like to speak to him, please.'

Lauren handed over the receiver and walked to the window to peer down at the dirt road, still eerily vacant except for two small dogs glowering and posturing in a show of dominance. The buildings and trees were rapidly losing substance in the swift tropical dusk. Deep and thick and velvety, it softened the raw intrusion of the buildings on the timeless tropical landscape.

Covertly eyeing Guy as he rattled off what sounded like a set of questions, she learned nothing from his face. He was, she thought warily, big in every way—tall and lithe and powerfully muscled, his wide shoulders and long legs backed up by an overpowering air of strength, both mental and physical.

Conversation concluded, he put the phone in his pocket and said in his almost perfectly accented English, 'Everything seems quiet there. The headman says the preacher is with his family high in the mountains—there has been a death.'

'So we can breathe again,' she said frivolously, shocked to realise how tense she'd been.

'I hadn't stopped,' he returned on a dry note, and opened the door.

Unclenching her teeth, Lauren preceded Guy out into the darkness, tossing words over her shoulder like hand grenades.

'I'm glad I can tell my friend that the nut-oil scheme seems to be working. It's great that the villagers get a reliable income from their land without having to fell the forests for lumber.' A little more steadily she added, 'I wish I could have seen what they're doing, though.'

Locking the door behind them, Guy responded with brutal frankness, 'They've got enough to worry about without trying to keep you safe. What are your plans now?'

Lauren looked at the single naked bulb that lit the stairwell. Fighting back a highly suspect—and dangerous—temptation to linger a few days at the resort, she said too promptly, 'I'll leave for New Zealand as soon as I can. Tomorrow, if I can get a seat on an outgoing plane.'

Guy startled her by unlocking the door again. 'You might, but don't bank on it. There are only two a day, not counting the twice-a-week flight to Valanu.'

'Where's Valanu? I've never heard of it. Is it another town on Sant'Rosa?'

'No.' Back in the office he picked up a telephone and punched in a few numbers. 'It's a scatter of islands to the south, part of another small Pacific nation.'

'The back of beyond, in other words.'

'Or paradise, depending on your outlook. It's a fair way off the beaten track,' he conceded, a disconcerting thread of mockery running through each word as he surveyed her with unreadable eyes and a tilted smile. 'But incredibly beautiful.' His voice lingered half a beat too long on the final word.

Colour tinged the skin along her cheekbones and an odd sensation twisted fiercely in the pit of her stomach. Swallowing, she switched her mind to her half-brother's holiday home in New Zealand, remote and lovely and utterly peaceful. Until she'd seen—until a short time ago, she amended swiftly, she'd been aching to get there.

And she still was. Jet lag had clouded her mind. As soon as she had some sleep she'd be her usual self. 'Who are you ringing?'

'The last flight to Atu will have just left, but someone should still be at the airfield. I'll book you a seat on the first plane out.'

Oddly piqued that he was so eager to get rid of her, she said lightly, 'Thank you so much.'

Someone *was* at the airfield, someone called Josef, with whom Guy conducted a conversation in the local language. When he hung up Lauren lifted her brows enquiringly.

'You've a seat reserved on tomorrow afternoon's flight,' he told her.

Formally, her smile set, she murmured, 'You've been very kind.'

His white teeth flashed in a grin. 'My pleasure,' he returned easily. 'Now, as the Chinese restaurant seems to be closed, we can go back to the resort and have dinner or I can take you home and feed you.'

'The resort,' Lauren said instantly, stopping when she realised that he'd tricked her. She met his amused eyes and thought with an entirely uncharacteristic rashness, Well, why not?

She was leaving tomorrow, so why shouldn't she share dinner with the most intriguing man she'd met for a long time? Utterly infuriating, of course—far too macho and high-handed and dominating—but since she'd seen him that dragging tiredness had been replaced by a swift, intoxicating excitement.

They had absolutely nothing in common, and when she was back home she'd wonder what it was about him that arced through her like an electrical charge, but for one night—one evening, she corrected herself hastily—she'd veer slightly towards the wild side. Every woman probably deserved a buccaneer experience once in her life.

But to make sure he didn't think he could lure her into his bed, she said, 'It won't be a late night, though— I've had two hours' sleep in the last twenty-four, and I'm running on empty.'

He understood the implication. Irony tinged his smile as he held open the door. 'I'll deliver you to your door within two minutes of the first yawn. Watch where you put your feet.'

The single bulb over the stairs flickered ominously as a huge moth came to rest on it. To the sound of their footsteps echoing on the bare concrete, Lauren gripped the pipe handrail and negotiated the stairs.

'Now that it's dark the air is fresher, even though it hasn't cooled down much,' she remarked sedately as they walked towards the Land Rover. 'I can smell the scent of the flowers without any underlying taint of decay.'

'That's the tropics—ravishing beauty and rotting vegetation,' Guy said unromantically, opening the vehicle door.

Lauren slid in, watching him walk around the front of the vehicle, tall and powerful in the weak light of the only street lamp. She felt exposed and tingling, as though meeting him had stripped away several skins to reveal a world of unsuspected excitement and anticipation.

Calm down, she warned herself. Heady recklessness is so *not* your thing.

She'd built a successful and satisfying life on discretion and discipline; she wasn't going to allow the tropics to cast any magic spell on her!

Halfway back to the resort, Guy said, 'It seems a pity to leave the South Coast without seeing our main claim to fame.'

'Which is?' she asked cautiously.

'A waterfall.'

Lauren paused. Maybe it was the soft radiance in the sky that proclaimed the imminent arrival of a full moon, but another rash impulse overrode common sense.

'All right,' she said, regretting the words the moment they left her mouth.

Guy swung the vehicle between two dark walls of trees; within seconds the unmarked road deteriorated into teeth-jolting ruts. Nevertheless, he skirted potholes with a nonchalant skill she envied. Clinging to the seat, she looked around uneasily; nightfall had transformed the lush vegetation into an alien, menacing entity that edged onto the track.

Watching large leaves whip by, she decided she'd been crazy to accept Guy's challenge—because challenge it had definitely been.

He pulled up beneath a huge tree, its heavy foliage drooping to the ground to make a kind of tent around the Land Rover. As he switched off the engine, Lauren groped for the handle and jumped out.

'This way,' he said crisply.

After a few yards the oppressive growth pulled back to reveal a swathe of coarse grass. Lauren's eyes grew accustomed to the darkness as they walked towards a steady soft murmur, infinitely refreshing, that whispered through the sticky air.

'Look,' Guy said, stopping.

Water fell from on high, a shimmering veil under the stars. Down the rock face clustered palms, their fronds edged with the promise of moonlight.

'It's beautiful,' she said softly. 'Oh— I didn't realise we were so close to the coast.'

The wide pool emptied over another lip of rock into a small stream that wound its way a few hundred yards to the sea. Through the feathery tops of the coconut palms she could see the white crescent of a beach and the oily stillness of a wide bay.

'I'm surprised there's no coral reef around the island,' she said, uncomfortably moved by the exquisite allure of the scene. It roused a wild longing she'd never experienced before—an urge to shuck off the trappings of civilisation and surrender to the potent seduction of the Pacific.

Guy told her, 'Not all South Sea islands have them. Right, it's just about time for the show. Look at the waterfall.'

The moon soared above the horizon, its light transforming the fall of water into a shimmering gold radiance.

'Oh!' she breathed. 'Oh, that is exquisite—like a fall of firelit silk! Thank you for bringing me here.'

When he didn't answer she looked up.

He was watching her, the bold structure of his face picked out by the moonlight. His mouth was compressed, and his high, faintly Slavic cheekbones gave him a half-wild, exotic air. He looked, she thought feverishly, like the buccaneer she'd likened him to before—merciless and utterly compelling. Tension flamed through her, driven by a rush of adrenaline that took her breath away.

Dry-mouthed and desperate, she swivelled away to fix her gaze on the quietly falling water, glowing with an iridescent mingling of gold and silver and copper, and tried to defuse the situation with words. 'It's such a familiar glory, isn't it, moonrise, and yet I get carried away by it each time. But I've never seen anything like this—it looks like cloth of gold, almost as though the light is coming through the water from the back.'

'As you say, a familiar miracle.' He took her arm and walked her across to the bank. The moonlight hadn't yet reached the pool; it gleamed before them, a shimmering circle of obsidian.

His touch cut through her defences, bypassing willpower, smashing her hard-won control to kindle fires in her flesh.

Dark magic, she thought despairingly. She ached to surrender to its terrifying temptation so much she could taste the craving, sweet and potent and desperate.

Staring into the smooth black water, she clenched her muscles against desire, forcing herself to freeze, not to turn into his arms and lift her face in mute invitation. He said nothing, but she heard his breathing alter, and tension spiralled between them, glittering and seductive. All it would take was one movement from her, and she'd know the power of his kiss and shiver at the warmth of his hands on her breasts...

'The stream comes from springs in the mountains, so the water is cold.' His voice was steady, yet a raw note grated beneath the matter-of-fact tone.

Heat spread from the pit of her stomach, a sweet, piercing flame that took no prisoners.

Cold water, she thought feverishly, just might do the trick, because this instant arousal had never happened to her before, and one-night stands were not her style. Stooping, she dipped her hand in, whipping it back with shock as it numbed her fingers. 'It's freezing!'

Something in his stillness alerted her; he seemed to loom over her, almost threatening. She scrambled up again and took a couple of hasty steps away, turning to watch the transient radiance of the waterfall fade as the moon leapt higher in the sky. Her blood pulsed heavily, filling her with this strange, exotic madness.

The tropics, she thought feverishly, were notorious for this sort of thing. *Get over it.*

'That is utterly beautiful,' she said, striving for a briskly practical tone. 'Thank you for bringing me here.'

'My pleasure,' he told her without expression. 'Shall we go?'

She nodded and they started back towards the tree that hid the Land Rover. A few steps beneath the overhanging branches, Guy stopped and listened, an intimidating shadow in the darkness of the canopy. Startled and uneasy, Lauren opened her mouth to ask what was going on, but the hard impact of his hand across her mouth stopped the words.

Oh God, she thought, struggling violently, you utter *moron*, Lauren Porter!

Hand still across her mouth, he hauled her into the thicker darkness and slammed her against the trunk, judging his strength so that although she was crushed breathless between his body and the unforgiving tree, she wasn't hurt. Imprisoned by his strength, she felt the iron strength of muscles flexed for action.

Think! she adjured herself, fighting the terror that tried to freeze her brain. Buying time and hoping to take him by surprise, she slumped against him and sucked in air, visualising just what she'd do to disable him.

His words pitched only for her ear, he said, 'I can hear voices, and I don't know who they are.'

Lauren strained to listen, but apart from the sweet singing of the waterfall she could hear nothing.

Eventually, still in that same chilling monotone, he said, 'Stay still and don't make a noise.'

Eyes enormous above the ruthless hand that compelled her silence, she nodded.

His grip relaxed. Instantly, fingers curving into claws, Lauren reached for his genitals and opened her mouth to scream.

His cruel hand stifled any sound. With lethal strength Guy quelled her struggles and pulled her against him, locking his other arm around her.

'Shut up!' he said in a low, fierce thread of a voice that terrified her anew.

When she tried to fight with her teeth and her nails, he shook her hard enough to jar her, then muttered, 'Listen, damn you! What can you hear?'

Above the softly lyrical music of the waterfall came voices. Male voices chanting something—the guttural rhythms becoming louder. Tension dried Lauren's mouth and drove more adrenaline into every cell. The primitive fear of assault and rape was replaced by an even more basic one—that of death.

Yet possibly they were just villagers out on a fishing trip, and Guy was making sure there'd be no witnesses to—to whatever he wanted to do.

She had an instant to make up her mind whether or not to trust him. Later she'd convince herself that her decision was based on sheer pragmatism—she'd have a better chance of survival if she had to deal with only one man.

Yet it was instinct that convinced her, not common sense or good judgement.

In her ear he murmured, 'Don't move, don't say anything.'

She nodded. Stealthily, slowly, he eased his hand

away from her mouth. In spite of his size he moved as silently as a cat, positioning himself with his back to her, shielding her, she realised, with his body from whatever danger lurked out there. Terrified for his safety, she took comfort from the steady pounding of his heart as her apprehension condensed into ice.

The voices receded, but still Guy stayed motionless.

She was stiff and shaking when at last he stepped away.

'Who—?' she whispered.

Guy's lethal, slashing gesture stopped the words in her throat. He was looking towards the sea; as she watched he moved with a fluid lack of noise to part the leaves on one of the branches that sheltered them.

Beneath his breath he said, 'There—yes. Can you see them?'

They were some distance away, but the moon shone on lithe oiled bodies, already almost on the beach. About twenty men, carrying what appeared to be spears.

'Out to sea,' Guy said quietly.

Narrowing her eyes, she squinted into the glare of the moon. Small black shapes seemed to be skipping across its path over the sea.

'Canoes?' she whispered.

'Dugouts. Banana boats, which have outboards, but they're not using them tonight. And they're coming from the wrong direction—heading towards the resort.' He made up his mind. 'Come on, we need to get out of here. Get into the Land Rover, but don't slam the door until I turn the engine on. Then lock it and keep down.'

Numbly, Lauren obeyed. As the vehicle burst from beneath the tree, she locked the door and prayed that no one lay in wait along that narrow, treacherous track.

Guy had the night sight of a predator; without headlights, he drove at high speed through the thick darkness, confidently following the track Lauren couldn't see. On the way to the waterfall she'd enjoyed the difference between the exotic vegetation and the woods she was accustomed to; now the jungle threatened, hiding who knew what danger.

'Do you think they were going to join the canoeists, or fight them?' she asked once they had left the waterfall and its black pool behind.

'I don't know, but that was a war chant,' he said curtly.

Fighting a sickening knot of fear, she swayed as the vehicle swung around corners and surged through potholes and ruts. A sense of danger—palpable and chillingly pervasive—settled around them. Once, in a small clearing, she caught a glimpse of Guy's profile against the moon, and a memory teased her mind with fugitive recognition.

She'd seen a photograph—and then the tantalising image vanished, wiped from her brain.

Where—and how—would she have seen a photograph of a beachcomber from Sant'Rosa?

He glanced at her and suddenly swore in a liquid language that sounded vaguely Italian before ordering, 'Pull my shirt out of my trousers.'

'What?'

He flashed her a feral grin. 'Contain yourself. You're showing far too much gleaming skin—far too obvious. Cover it with my shirt.'

'But that leaves you exposed.'

'I'm much darker than you, so I'm harder to see.' The amusement was gone; this time it was an order. 'Pull the shirt out from my waistband and haul it up over the arm furthest from you; I'll tell you when to drag it over my head.'

'Surely stopping—'

'I'm not stopping,' he said quietly. 'I don't know who else might be around. Get the shirt off.'

Lauren gritted her teeth as her questing fingers skidded over sleek skin padded with muscle. Once his arm had been freed she waited, the material gathered in her hand.

'There's a straight length of road— OK, haul it over my head. *Now!*'

She jerked the soft, warm garment over his head in one smooth movement.

'Get it off my other arm—now!' he barked.

He made it easy for her, lithely shrugging free of the shirt. 'Now cover yourself,' he ordered in a tone that lifted every tiny hair on her body upright.

Silently she hauled it over her head, shivering as the material settled around her shoulders. The faint scent of his skin—vital, potent—almost banished the metallic taste of fear in her mouth.

Guy commanded, 'Crouch down on the floor and stay there until I tell you to get out. Cover your face and your hands. If we stop, don't move unless I tell you to. If we get stopped, don't say anything—try not to breathe.'

The ice beneath her ribs expanding, she obeyed, folding herself into the foot well and praying that the maverick instinct to trust him hadn't played her false. 'Those men were aiming for the resort, weren't they?'

He didn't try to evade the truth. 'That was the direction they were heading towards.'

'Do you think there might be violence?'

When he didn't answer immediately she said with

sharp emphasis, 'I'm not going to faint or scream or panic.'

The swift flash of his grin reassured her. 'I believe you.' But the momentary spark of humour dissolved into grimness as he swerved to avoid some small animal scurrying across the road.

Lauren braced herself, wincing as her elbow hit the floor.

He went on calmly, 'What their leader—or leaders—plan, I have no idea. If they find the resort empty, they'll probably take what they want, get drunk on the contents of the bar, then go back home.'

She nodded. 'How long will it take us to get to the resort?'

'We're not going there,' he said, changing gear.

CHAPTER THREE

'WHAT?' When he didn't answer she demanded, 'Why not?'

'Because I'm taking you straight to the airport,' he said above the snarl of the engine.

Lauren peered up at an angular jaw harshly outlined against the radiant moonlight. She pitched her voice louder. 'But we have to warn them.'

'They'll have been warned. The jungle might look empty, but there are eyes everywhere, which is why you're sitting on the floor now.' He shot a swift glance at her shocked face. 'Worrying about them isn't going to achieve anything; I'm not going back to the resort.'

Appalled, she demanded, 'But—what about the children?'

'Leave it,' he bit back, his voice coldly adamant. 'The resort's in direct contact with the police—the staff will have evacuated the tourists as soon as they got the word.'

'And if it isn't just a ragtag and bobtail group of cargo cultists who want European-style beds and television sets?' she almost shouted. 'If they're armed and they mean mayhem, what then?'

He concentrated on steering at heart-shocking speed around a tight corner. 'Once we've got you all out of the way, we'll deal with whatever happens.'

Lauren huddled uncomfortably against the seat, wondering if people were crouching in ambush with rifles and machetes. She was, she realised, afraid, but not terrified; somehow Guy exuded an aura of such authority that she trusted him to get them out of whatever situation they were in.

Something he'd said clicked. She blurted, 'You're planning to stay and fight, aren't you?' When he didn't answer she persisted, 'Why? Are you Sant'Rosan?'

'No,' he said curtly, a total lack of compromise in his tone. 'But I know the people and I've got a lot invested in Sant'Rosa— *Get right down!*'

Before she could react, he swore and thrust her forcefully beneath the dash as he applied the brakes. The vehicle slammed to a stop.

Crouched in a heap, her heart jumping so noisily she was sure it could be heard above the noise of the engine, Lauren heard rough, angry male voices. In spite of the thick heat, she shivered and tried to slow down the quick, shallow pants of her breathing.

Calmly Guy answered, his voice level and without fear. When someone laughed Lauren relaxed slightly, glancing up as Guy asked a question. Harsh yellow light—a spotlight?—traced the sweep of his cheekbones; she recalled the Slavic horsemen who had ridden into Europe over a millennium ago, and wondered just what his ancestry was.

Someone said something that made him frown and fire another question. He looked so confident and completely in charge of the situation that she was startled when she saw his lean fingers tighten on the steering wheel. His next remark produced much more laughter; he grinned and added a few words that brought a babble of comment.

Oh, how she wished she understood the language! Fluency in French and German amounted to nothing in this turbulent part of the world.

Although her body soon began to complain, she didn't dare move a muscle, not even when the vehicle started and they drove off to a chorus of deep farewells.

'All right,' Guy said a few minutes later, 'we're out of sight. You can sit up, but keep your head down.'

Stiffly she uncurled, stretching her arms. 'Who were they?'

'A police patrol, but they warned that there are roving bands of possible looters in the bush so we won't take any chances. The resort's been cleared—the guests are at the airport.'

Well, at least they'd be safe there, and she'd be able to resume her journey to New Zealand.

She said, 'I'm so glad they're all right.' And then remembered something. 'But you said there are no flights until tomorrow morning.'

'Josef, the manager, has managed to radio a pilot who's doing a chartered freight trip to Valanu from the Republic,' Guy said briefly. 'He's prepared to take everyone. You'll be sitting in the aisles, but you'll get there.' The note of the engine deepened as the vehicle picked up speed. 'The only problem is, he wants to leave as soon as possible, so brace yourself. I've got twenty minutes to get you to the airport.'

Valanu? She frowned, then remembered what he'd called the place. *A scatter of islands...*

Her breath hissed out. 'But why Valanu? Can't he fly us to the capital?'

'Communication with the rest of Sant'Rosa has been cut.'

'Why?'

'I don't know, but it's almost certainly nothing to do with this business.' His voice was reassuring. 'Communications here are erratic at the best of times—it's probably a coincidence.'

Lauren digested this. 'Will the mine be safe?'

'Against anything smaller than an army, yes. They have their own security, but they're too far away to help us.'

He swung the vehicle around a corner, and after that there was no further chance to talk. Lauren was unclenching her jaw muscles for about the fifth time when above the sound of the engine she heard something else—a sudden outbreak of loud pops.

Guy said something under his breath in the language she didn't recognise.

'What was that?' she asked, afraid she knew the answer.

'Gunfire,' he said laconically. 'And that means serious trouble.'

Lauren's stomach dropped endlessly.

He glanced briefly down. 'Relax, I'll keep you safe.'

Lauren didn't doubt that; what frightened her was the possibility of him being hurt. And that was strange, because she barely knew the man. OK, so he had a bewildering effect on her, but she didn't even like him much, although he'd been kind in his arrogant way. Apart from common humanity, why should she care about his safety?

'Here we are,' he said at last. He killed the engine and looked around with the curiously still intentness of a predator sensing prey, before ordering curtly, 'Stay there.'

A swift, silent rush took him out of the Land Rover and around to her door. When it opened Lauren pulled herself onto the seat, groaning beneath her breath when her cramped legs protested painfully.

Strong hands caught her by the waist; as he lifted her out and set her down, Guy said, 'You did well. I'm sorry you got caught up in this.'

Her legs refused to carry her; when she staggered, he lifted her and strode off towards the dim figure waiting outside the small terminal building.

From here the gunfire seemed harmless, more like fireworks. Locked in Guy's safe, strong arms with the moon silvering his bare shoulders, Lauren hoped fervently that no one was dying out there—and desperately that the raiders would be repelled by the time Guy left the airport.

The waiting man gestured, saying something urgently. Lauren felt Guy tense, before he rattled out a question.

The answer didn't please him. He replied in a quiet, deadly voice and put Lauren down, supporting her with an arm around her shoulders. The man stepped back swiftly to usher them both into the reception area.

Tiny, it was almost filled with the resort guests, several carrying children who cried or stared around with bewildered eyes. Suitcases were being shuffled onto an elderly cart, and everyone looked strained and serious.

The man who had met them glanced at Lauren and switched to English. 'Passport, please, ma'am.'

Lauren said shakily, 'It's back at the resort. In the safe with my ID—with all my papers.'

The solid, middle-aged man whose glossy dark hair was greying at the temples looked shocked. 'I'm sorry, ma'am, but—'

'Josef, this is no time for formalities,' Guy interrupted, his deep voice harsh. 'You know she can't stay here.'

A uniformed man—the pilot, Lauren realised—strode

swiftly in from the other side of the building. 'Guy!' he said, grinning largely, 'I might have guessed you'd be here! No show without Punch, eh?' He examined Lauren with interest.

Guy acknowledged the greeting and concisely told him what had happened.

The pilot frowned. 'Man, I can't take her to Valanu without papers! You know they won't let her in— they've been paranoid ever since that drug syndicate tried to infiltrate.'

'You'll take her,' Guy said curtly. 'There's no alternative.'

Frowning, his voice tight with concern, Josef interposed, 'She cannot travel to Valanu without papers.'

In a voice that could have splintered granite, Guy said, 'She'll leave Sant'Rosa if I have to hijack Brian's plane.'

The pilot looked at Lauren's startled face and away again. 'You know what they'll do with her, Guy. They'll chuck her in prison with the prostitutes and the addicts, and she won't get out until someone vouches for her or she gets new papers. In Valanu that could take weeks—everything goes through Fiji. Now, if it was you, Guy, it would be OK. They know you—they'd let you in without a passport.'

Lauren said, 'Look, it's all right. Don't worry about me.'

All three men stared at her with identical expressions, and then at each other.

'Don't be stupid,' Guy said brusquely.

Naked from the waist up, with light gleaming gold on his broad, tanned shoulders and strongly muscled arms, he looked like a barbaric warrior, his unshaven face only emphasising his formidable presence.

Between his teeth he said, 'Josef, you're a pastor in your church, aren't you?'

Josef glanced at him with astonishment. 'I am,' he agreed.

'Very well, then. You can marry us and I'll vouch for her.'

The pilot gave a crack of laughter. 'Yep, that'd do it. Trust you, Guy, to come up with the goods.' He glanced at his watch. 'But you'd better tie that knot as soon as you can. I'm leaving in ten minutes. That gunfire's getting closer.'

Stunned, Lauren gasped, 'That's utterly impossible. I don't even know your name.'

'Guy Bagaton,' Guy said indifferently, adding with brutal candour, 'And you don't have a choice.' He nodded at the airport manager. 'All right, Josef, let's get it over and done with.'

A ragged salvo of popping noises silenced everyone in the terminus. It faded away, to be followed by a heavy *whoomph* that seemed to lift the ground beneath their feet. One of the women stifled a scream and a child started to whimper. With a muffled oath, the pilot raced out of the building.

The harassed Sant'Rosan marshalling the passengers had jumped along with everyone else, but recovered himself quickly. 'Please, board in a line. Women and children first, please.'

The small crowd clumped into a disorderly file and began to follow the pilot across the grass airstrip.

Guy said shortly, 'Josef, get going! We don't have time to waste.' He took Lauren's elbow in a grip that meant business and urged her after the manager, already heading into a small office.

Once there, Josef said, 'I am a minister in my church

here, but perhaps such a marriage will not be legal any-where but on Sant'Rosa. However, ma'am, it will mean that you will get out of here and they will not put you in prison in Valanu.'

Lauren protested, 'No! Look, prison can't be that bad—and it shouldn't take long to get another passport from Britain. Anyway, how do you know they'll let me in even if I do go ahead with this?'

'Trust me,' Guy answered, his expression grimly determined, 'they will. And trust me again—tropical prisons are more than unhygienic, and it could take weeks to replace your papers—always assuming the Valanuan authorities let you contact the British representative in Fiji.' The hard authority in his tone and the granite cast of his features silenced her objection. 'Just say yes in all the right places, otherwise you'll be caught in a war zone. If that happens, you'll endanger anyone who has to look after you.'

It was that final truth that convinced her. White-lipped, she said, 'What are you going to do?'

'Don't worry about me.'

Nightmarish images from television screens clouded her mind so that she couldn't think beyond a silent, urgent plea that he stay safe.

'Don't worry,' he said, a cynical edge to the words. 'The marriage will satisfy the bureaucracy on Valanu that you're not a beachcomber intent on drinking and drugging the rest of your life away at their expense.' He drew the gold signet ring from his little finger and turned her to face Josef.

Numbly, Lauren went through with the brief ceremony, backed by the sound of the plane's engines and punctuated by the ominous sound of gunfire and a couple more of those heavy explosions.

She responded like an automaton, shivering when Guy slid the ring onto her finger, holding it there because it was too big. Warm from his body heat, it felt like a shackle, but she relaxed a little as he gripped her hand in his strong one.

At last Josef said, 'You may kiss the bride,' and tactfully busied himself with the papers.

A marauder's smile played across Guy's sensual mouth. Eyes gleaming, he murmured, 'If I'd known I was going to get married today, I'd have shaved.'

Then he kissed her—not a swift, parting kiss, nor a clumsy, unsubtle expression of lust. His mouth took hers in complete mastery, replacing every fear with poignant delight and a swift, fierce longing that lodged in her heart.

And because she didn't know whether he'd survive, whether she'd ever see him again, she kissed him back with everything she had to give.

Too soon, he released her with an odd half-smile to scribble a name on a piece of paper. 'My agent on Valanu,' he said, handing it to her. 'Get in touch with him straight away and show him the papers Josef's making out now—he'll find you a place to stay. You have no money?'

'No,' she said wretchedly, feeling empty and oddly weepy.

He wrenched a wallet from his pocket and took out the notes in it. 'This will cover your costs for tonight.' He handed them over, adding with wry humour, 'And there's enough there to buy you another sarong from the market.'

'Your shirt!'

One hand clenched around the notes and his ring, she

began to jerk his T-shirt upwards, but he said, 'Keep it on. It gives you that authentic refugee look.'

She hesitated, then let the material fall. 'What will you wear?'

'I will lend him one of mine,' Josef said sombrely.

Guy's intent, uncompromising scrutiny drowned her in tawny fire. 'I'll contact you as soon as I can.'

'P-promises,' she said, sudden tears blinding her.

He laughed and picked up her free hand, kissing the back and then the palm, folding her fingers over to keep the kiss there. 'I always keep my promises.' It sounded like a vow.

'Come, ma'am,' Josef said earnestly. 'The plane is ready.'

'Go now,' Guy said, and strode out into the darkness without a backward glance.

An hour later, as the engines droned above the dark, empty ocean, Lauren twisted the gold signet ring on her finger, and wondered what was happening back on Sant'Rosa.

'Keep him safe,' she whispered.

And with the stars swallowed up by the moon's light, and the white circle of Valanu's biggest atoll on the horizon, she tried to forget that somewhere behind her a stranger, a man she had only met that day, might be fighting for his life.

And tried very hard to convince herself that she hadn't fallen in love in three short hours.

The ceiling fan whirred, wafting a sluggish wave of clammy air over Lauren's head. Gathering her dignity, she said, 'So I can't leave Valanu yet.'

Regretfully the immigration official shook his head. 'I am afraid not,' he agreed. 'It is complicated, you see.

You came here without papers; we let you in as a favour because you are married to a man who has a good name in this place.' He tapped the file on his desk. 'But it is taking longer than we expected to get replacement papers from Britain, and until then you cannot leave Valanu because our only air link to the outside world is Sant'Rosa, and they say they will not allow you to land there without a passport.'

'My parents said my passport had been sent by courier two days ago.'

They had had variations on the same conversation for the past six afternoons. Tension plucked Lauren's nerves, but screaming wouldn't achieve anything. Everyone had been utterly polite, very helpful—and determined to stick to the rules.

Guy had been right. With no British consulate, all official matters had to go through the distant island nation that ruled Valanu, so she was stuck on this lovely, isolated atoll until proof of her identity and citizenship arrived.

Guy's agent might have been able to speed things up, but he'd flown to Singapore the day before she'd arrived on Valanu and wasn't expected back for several more days.

Fortunately the clerk at Valanu's airport who'd converted Guy's notes to the local currency had asked her where she was staying. When she'd admitted she had nowhere, he'd recommended his cousin's place, and half an hour later she'd rented a one-room bungalow standing on a coral platform in a tangle of foliage and sweet-smelling flowers.

She pasted a smile to her face and got to her feet. 'Thank you very much for all your help.'

'I'm sorry I can't make things happen more quickly

for you, but I hope you are enjoying our little island.'
He paused, before saying carefully, 'It is a possibility
that if you spoke to one of the journalists trying to get
to Sant'Rosa, they might be able to help you contact
your family in England.'

God, no! Lauren had been carefully avoiding them
for the past few days. Not that she was interesting to
the media, except for the fact that she was Marc
Corbett's half-sister, and Marc was a player on the
world stage. She didn't want anyone poking around in
the past and discovering the secret of her mother's long-
ago affair with Marc's father. Apart from humiliating
her mother, any publication of that indiscretion would
stress her father, whose health was precarious.

She held out her hand. 'I'm enjoying my time on
Valanu, and you've been most kind,' she told the official truthfully. 'I'm just worried about what's happening
on Sant'Rosa.'

Sombre-faced, he shook her hand. 'Yes,' he said
heavily. 'War is a terrible thing, and it is so sad to see
the Sant'Rosans suffering again. However, if what we
are hearing is correct, the invaders are already being
pushed back beyond the border and their ringleader is
dead.'

Rumour or truth? 'I hope so,' she said in a flat voice.

Slowly, because the late-afternoon sun beat down
with unmitigated ferocity, she walked to her bungalow.
Once in its blessed coolness, she poured a glass of water
from the jug in the tiny refrigerator and stood slowly
sipping it in the minuscule kitchen.

Beneath the high, thatched roof, a huge bed draped
in mosquito netting dominated the room; although
Lauren slept with only a sheet over her, the coverlet
was a work of art, brilliantly quilted in a pattern of

hibiscus flowers. With a table and chairs, the only other furniture was a wardrobe that held Guy's shirt—washed and pressed and awaiting his arrival—and the spare sarong she'd bought the morning after she'd been decanted from the plane.

During the day the woven mats that made the walls were rolled up so that sea breezes cooled the building; at night, they provided privacy.

Spartan, she thought, draining the glass with relief, but clean and comfortable; more importantly, it was cheap. The call she'd made to her parents in England had used so much of Guy's money that she'd had to watch every penny, haggling for fish and fruit in the market. With funds from home apparently wending their way via outer space, she'd soon be forced to borrow from Guy's agent when he returned from Singapore.

Apart from her daily trek to report to the immigration officer, she swam, prepared meals and chatted to her landlady's teenage daughters, trying to satisfy their curiosity about life outside their idyllic island. Unfortunately, such a lazy life gave her too much time to imagine Guy Bagaton dead...

Even though death was no respecter of persons, it was impossible to imagine all that vibrant power cut down by a bullet—or worse.

'He'll be fine,' she said aloud. She had the oddest feeling that if he died she'd know.

'You don't even know *him*,' she scoffed, and went down to the lagoon to swim off the dust and the sweat of the walk home.

The water lapped against her like liquid silk, soothing and lukewarm, but a blood-red sky to the west heralded the sunset, turning her white skin copper as she strolled back along the beach. It seemed ominous, a bad omen.

'Grow up,' she chided, slipping off her sandals at the door. 'You are not superstitious.'

Once inside she showered and washed her salt-laden hair before changing into her other sarong, a splashy print of gorgeous, improbably coloured frangipani blooms. Thanks to the landlady's daughters, she now knew three ways of tying the garment. This time she settled for a simple knot above her breasts before sitting on the side of the bed to comb her hair. As the teeth smoothed through each strand, a feather of awareness stroked along her skin.

Several times she looked around, but the tangle of growth that surrounded the bungalow was empty of prying eyes. Anyway, it wasn't the sort of sensation that whispered of danger. More a feeling of languorous expectancy, as though something good was going to happen...

'Perhaps your new passport will arrive tomorrow,' she murmured, looking down at her clenched hand; because she wasn't married, she'd taken to wearing Guy's signet ring on her middle finger. It was still too big, but it didn't slip off.

It was made of heavy gold, and the engraving almost worn away; not for the first time, she turned her hand in the red light of the dying sun, trying to make out its form. Some sort of crest, she thought—a bird? Were those wings? The outline danced in the smoky light and she blinked hard to clear her sight, but had to give up again.

Whatever, he clearly valued it, so when she finally got off Valanu she'd leave it with the agent.

Driven by restlessness, she let down the woven sides

of the room and loosened the knot on her sarong, walking out onto the coral platform to enjoy the cooler air of evening on her bare shoulders and arms. A yawn took her by surprise.

'What the *hell* are you doing here?' a familiar voice enquired from behind.

CHAPTER FOUR

ONE hand holding back her heartbeats, Lauren swung around. A large dark silhouette against the violent crimson of the sky, Guy Bagaton stood a few feet away.

Relief and incandescent joy rioted through her, shocking her with their intensity.

Guy demanded, 'Why aren't you staying at the resort?'

'I didn't have enough money,' she told him, fighting to keep her voice level. Although he stood about ten feet away, his awareness rested like a blade against her sensitised skin. 'Your agent is in Singapore—he's expected back tomorrow.'

Guy said something that made her brows shoot up. 'So what have you been using for money? The amount I gave you wouldn't have kept you for a week.'

'It has,' she said.

Then her eyes adjusted to the rapidly fading light, and she gasped and raced towards him. *'What happened?'*

He ignored the bandage around his upper arm. 'It's nothing—a crease from a bullet,' he said curtly. 'How are you?'

'I'm fine.' Brows drawn together, she examined him closely.

He was still villainously unshaven, his autocratic features were more deeply carved, and something in his eyes—a kind of bitter determination, as though he'd

56

kept going through events that no one should ever see—
had dimmed his tremendous vitality.

Empathy twisted her heart into a hard knot in her
chest. No man should look like that. 'How did you
know I was here?'

He sent her a stabbing glance. 'It took me a while.
In the end I called in a favour from someone who works
in the immigration service.' He looked around. 'This is
no place for you.'

'Has a doctor looked at that bullet crease?'

'Yes. She jabbed me and provided me with antibi-
otics. It's barely a scratch.' He held out a plastic bag
and, when Lauren automatically took it without stopping her anxious scrutiny of his face, commented drily,
'You can open it. Your passport is in there.'

'My passport!' Hastily she pulled the bag open and
saw the familiar cover. She looked up again sharply.
'Did you go back to the resort?'

His lashes drooped. 'Briefly. It had been looted, but
they hadn't been able to get into the safe.'

The hairs on the back of Lauren's neck lifted.
'How—was everybody all right?'

'There was no one there, but as far as I know, the
staff survived.' He finished, 'The passport's intact and
unblemished.'

Gratefully she said, 'Thank you so much. It was ter-
ribly kind of you to take the trouble.'

Yet all she could think was that it meant she could
now leave Valanu—when he had just arrived. A dangerously heady enchantment wrapped her with silken
energy.

Lust, she thought, yet knew she was wrong. At the
beginning, yes—it had been stark, undiluted animal attraction—but now she knew much more about Guy

Bagaton, and that physical chemistry had transmuted into something she didn't dare examine. He had saved her from what could have been her death; she wished she could help him with the cocktail of emotions simmering beneath his granite façade.

She put her passport on the table, its familiar formality incongruous amongst the scarlet taffeta of a cluster of hibiscus flowers. 'Come in—no, let's sit outside; it's slightly cooler.'

True, but it was also less intimate. Babbling slightly, she continued, 'You look as though you could do with a drink—a previous guest left behind a couple of cans of beer if you want some. They're still in the fridge.'

He said on a harsh half-laugh, 'You're a woman out of every man's fantasy.'

A rill of pleasure ran through her, hotly disturbing. Getting a can, she said lightly, 'Because I offered you a beer? You've got remarkably low standards if that's all a woman has to do.'

He took it from her, broke the seal, and drank half the contents in one swallow. Lauren busied herself pouring a long glass of tangy fruit juice before turning to find him watching her with a narrow-eyed intensity that almost sent her swaying into his arms.

'Nothing like a can of beer after a few days' fighting in the jungle,' he said after a second so taut she could feel its impact twanging along her nerves.

Lauren let her breath go on a noiseless sigh. 'Let's sit on the terrace.'

He sank into one of the chairs with a sigh that hinted of bone-deep weariness. 'Did you have any problems getting into Valanu?'

'At first they didn't want to let me off the plane.' She drank the juice, taste buds purring at its acidic tang, every sense honed and on tiptoe. 'The fake marriage papers—and the pilot—persuaded them to relent. He stayed long enough to convince them that I was truly married to you.'

'Beachcombers are a damned nuisance in the Pacific. Without tough policies for keeping them out, the islands would have freeloaders from all over the world preying on the locals. Who have little enough for themselves, most of the time.'

'Your name did the trick.' She wanted very much to know what had happened on Sant'Rosa, but instinct warned her not to probe. 'And you can't believe how grateful I am to you for thinking of it. I walked past the prison the other day, and you were right, it didn't look like a place I'd enjoy staying in.' Remembering how he'd tried to put her off going up to the village in the mountains, she finished with a hint of humour, 'I'll bet the cockroaches there are truly outstanding specimens.'

'No toenail is safe,' he agreed gravely and swallowed another mouthful of beer. The warm light of the lamp emphasised the lines engraved down his cheeks and the dark fans of the lashes hiding his eyes.

Fighting a disturbing urge to cradle his head against her breasts, Lauren averted her gaze to a sky so deeply black it was like staring into the heart of darkness. Stars began to wink into life, huge, impersonal, the pure air cutting the familiar cheerful twinkle.

Pitching her words just above the soft murmur of the waves, she asked, 'How long are you here for?'

The silence stretched so long she thought he'd gone to sleep.

Finally, in a voice completely without emotion, he said, 'It's over; there's a bit of mopping up still to do, but the preacher's followers have slunk back to their villages and the invaders have either been killed or fled back across the border. Sant'Rosan forces are in control.'

Not exactly an answer. 'It must have been bad,' she ventured.

He lifted the can and took another deep swallow of its contents. 'Bad enough,' he said flatly. 'About eighty people died—mostly villagers who got in the way. Crops destroyed and villages burned down, the bodies of dead children—the usual aftermath of war.'

'I'm sorry,' she said inadequately, her heart contracting.

'Why? It wasn't your fault.'

After a short silence she drawled, 'Are you looking for someone to blame?'

His quiet, mirthless laugh chilled her. He drained the rest of his beer, then stood up. 'Probably,' he said roughly. 'I'd better go; I'm in no fit state to discuss life and its unfairness with a gently brought-up Englishwoman.'

'Have you a place to go to?' She was teetering on the brink of something that would change her life, but she couldn't let him take his memories back to an impersonal hotel room.

'I'll get a room at the resort,' he said indifferently.

'And face a pack of ravening journalists who haven't been able to get anywhere near the fighting?' she returned, keeping her tone light. 'Although if the fighting's over, I suppose they've all left for Sant'Rosa. When did you eat last?'

He didn't answer straight away, and she suspected that her question had startled him. It had startled her too.

His broad shoulders lifted. 'God knows.'

'I'll get you something.' She got to her feet, strangely unsurprised to realise she'd made a decision—one, she thought with a flare of panic, that was totally unlike her. But her voice remained steady when she added, 'And while I'm doing that, why don't you have a shower?'

He didn't move. Although her eyes were attuned to the night, she couldn't see enough of his face to discern any expression, but his stance and his silence were intimidating.

Not so intimidating as his voice. Deep and raw, almost menacing, it sent a cold sliver of sensation down her spine. 'Not a good idea, Lauren.'

The darkness wasn't a barrier to him. When she flinched in humiliation, he cupped a lean hand around her chin. Applying the slightest pressure, he said without apology, 'I'm not fit company. I probably need to get drunk.'

His hand was warm, the long fingers rough as though he'd been working hard, the strength of it palpable against her skin. She said crisply, 'Then you'd regret it less tomorrow if you start out clean, and with some food in your stomach.'

'Indeed, a woman out of every man's fantasy,' he said in a voice like rough velvet.

His thumb stroked across her lips in a caress that melted her bones so that when he dropped his hand she had to grab the back of her chair.

But there was nothing caressing in the gaze that held hers. It was hot and dark and devouring; it reached into the hidden depths of thoughts and emotions she'd never recognised, never experienced before, and made her face them. 'But I'm not staying unless you're sure.'

Sure that she wanted to be with him? Utterly. Sure that she was ready for what might happen? No, but

certain that if she sent him to the resort she'd regret it.
'I'm sure.'

He nodded and stepped back, letting her go first into
the bungalow. Lauren switched on the light at the door,
and opened the wardrobe door to hand him the shirt
he'd lent her so many days ago. Tawny eyes quizzical,
he took it.

But when she drew the ring from her finger, his gaze
darkened. Her finger felt cold, abandoned, but her hand
didn't shake as she held out the gold trinket. 'Thank
you.'

'Is that what your offer is? Gratitude for getting your
passport? Or for getting you out of Sant'Rosa?' His tone
was softly aggressive, and he watched her so narrowly
she felt that her every thought was being catalogued by
that keen mind.

'No,' she said.

Guy slid the ring onto his little finger and went into
the bathroom.

He stayed for so long that Lauren, preparing a meal
of fish and salad in the kitchen, wondered whether he
was indulging in a ritual of cleaning war's filthy detritus
from his body.

It wouldn't be so easy or so quick to rid his mind of
the horrendous images.

She listened to the soft swish of the tiny waves brush-
ing the sand a few feet away and tried to sort out her
emotions. Send him off to the resort, common sense
urged. Now—before it's too late.

But it was too late. He'd issued a challenge and she'd
accepted it. Beneath Guy's tight control she sensed a
darkly primitive hunger; remember the traditional rec-
reation of the warrior, she thought—banishing unbearable memories in the pleasure of a woman's body.

But she didn't fear him; instinct told her that he wouldn't hurt her. And she wanted him with a heated desperation that fogged her mind, turning the unthinkable into the inevitable.

Oh, she could blame the heat and danger of the tropics—the perfume floating on the moist air, a sultry, sinful fragrance breathed out from the hearts of the crimson flowers on the vine wreathing the terrace. But the tropics hadn't produced the smouldering intensity that sent the blood singing through her veins.

Her teeth gnawed her lip as she went on with the dinner preparations. She wanted Guy, but even more important than that, she suspected that tonight he needed her.

When he emerged, clad in the clean shirt and his trousers, she was sitting on the terrace with the second can of beer and a plate of sliced fruit. She didn't hear him come up behind her, but some instinct switched her gaze from the geckos creeping ever closer to the lamp, intent on picking off the moths that danced in dazzled swirls around the dangerous, alluring light.

Her heart blocked her throat. He'd shaved, and in the soft light he was beautiful, the boldly carved framework of his face a miraculous, exotic blend of Mediterranean machismo and the northern-European angularity that nagged at her memory.

'That food looks good.' His voice was cool and non-committal.

He didn't fall on it like a starving man, but by the time he'd told her of the situation in Sant'Rosa he'd almost cleared the platter.

When he finished she observed, 'So the Republic *was* behind it. Are they likely to try again?'

'I don't think so. They lost too many men.'

She said quietly, 'And if they don't know by now that they can't ignore world opinion, they will once the Press gets there.'

'I'm surprised that a local fracas, however bloody and determined, was interesting enough to attract the attention of foreign correspondents.' His tone was satiric. 'There can't be much happening in the rest of the world.'

'A meeting of heads of state has just finished in Australia.' She looked up as a plane flew overhead.

'Ah, so that's it,' Guy said sardonically. 'And Sant'Rosa is an interesting detour on the way home. As for waking the world up to what's happening here—it'll be relegated to obscurity once the next flashpoint explodes.'

Unfortunately he was right. She said, 'I'd like to be sure that the hotel staff on Sant'Rosa survived. And how did the village in the mountains fare? It was right in the thick of things, surely?'

'No. As far as I know they didn't come off any worse than any other village. You're not going back,' Guy responded in a flat, lethal tone.

A cold shiver scudded down her spine. 'But—'

'No buts,' he said implacably. 'You won't be allowed anywhere near the South Coast. It's still a sensitive area. Civilians and sightseers—even well-intentioned ones— are nothing but a damned nuisance in a post-war zone unless they've got skills to help the victims.'

'Are you going back?' She held her breath until he answered.

'Yes.'

Something about his intonation and the formidable expression made her say, 'Why? What skills do you have to help?'

His left brow rose, as mocking as the smile that curved his mouth. 'I have contacts—I know who to apply to for the kind of aid that's needed, and I can act as go-between.'

An odd, aching foreboding clutched her with a cold grip. Ignoring it, she got to her feet and said, 'Dinner's ready. I'll go and get it.'

Over the meal Lauren set herself to switch Guy's mind away from the horrors of the past few days. She filled him in on the latest headlines, culled from the newspaper stand outside the immigration office, then skimmed over a couple of juicy financial scandals and the spectacularly spicy meltdown of a singer's marriage.

He knew what she was doing, but he went along with her and by the end of the meal he was laughing and the lines of tension scoring his lean face were slightly less deep.

Whereas she was now racked by taut expectancy.

'Coffee?' she asked, shielding herself with the banal little rituals of everyday life. 'It's only instant, I'm afraid.'

'It'll be fine.' He yawned and rubbed the back of his neck, the easy flexion of his big body sending a shivering little ripple of anticipation through her. 'But before you make it, I'll go and collect the other parcel I have for you.'

'What—'

'You'll see,' he said coolly.

It took him about twenty minutes, the longest twenty minutes of Lauren's life. When he came back she was sitting out on the terrace waiting for him, the friendly darkness pressing against her.

'Here,' he said, tossing a parcel onto the table.

'Oh.' Another plastic bag. 'What is it?'

'Clothes.'

Her clothes from Sant'Rosa. She said, 'Thank you. I thought they'd have been looted.'

'They're new.' He paused, then said, 'I should go.' He spoke abruptly, the words falling stark and curt in the heavy air.

Lauren got up and walked across to the tiny kitchen. With her back to him she filled the battered electric kettle and plugged it in, then set two cups on a tray with sugar and milk. Only when she'd made the coffee and picked up the tray did she ask coolly, 'Why?'

Guy watched her carry the tray across to the table. She walked as he'd dreamed of her in the hot, foetid jungle nights—with the lithe, easy grace that set off her long, lovely legs and the sensuous little sway of her hips that had dragged him temporarily out of hell.

He waited until she'd sat down and picked up the milk jug before saying in a deliberately prosaic voice, 'Because if I stay it will be in your bed, and I doubt if either of us will sleep much.'

Guy regretted the words as soon as they left his mouth. Pragmatism was doing its best to convince him that making love to a woman he'd forced into a temporary marriage was a stupid thing to do.

For once, pragmatism could go bury itself.

Her hand shook so much she had to set the milk jug down. She kept her head down too so that all he could see was the lovely curve of her cheekbone. After a moment she poured the milk in, then got up and turned off the lights.

In the soft half-darkness, illuminated only by the stars, she said quietly, 'I wouldn't have asked you to stay if I hadn't wanted that.'

Damn it, he could taste the need, hot as sin, dangerously heady as any drug; wanting Lauren was an ache in his guts, a reckless loss of control that both excited and infuriated him.

And for the first time in his life he was being propositioned by a woman who had no idea who he was. Here in Valanu they knew him only as Guy Bagaton. Combined with the heated sexual appetite raging through him, Lauren's offer was damned near irresistible.

'Neither reward nor gratitude,' Lauren said.

Was there a hint of nervousness beneath the polished surface? When she stopped a step away, Guy refused to reach out, although the muscles in his shoulders and arms bunched with the effort to keep them still. Leaping on her with famished savagery was not the way to endear yourself to a woman, he thought derisively.

He asked, 'So what is it?'

The taut seconds that followed his question didn't give him enough time to impose control on his more primitive instincts. He could die wanting her, he thought, grimly fighting the physical longing that undermined his will-power, but he hadn't come here for this.

Then she bent and fitted her mouth to his. Against his lips she said, 'This.'

And kissed him.

She tasted of mystery and delight, of sex and truth, of daring and intensity and grace. An exultant, desperate need roared through him, and he said too harshly, 'Good, because that's what I want too.'

When Lauren began to straighten, he came up with her in a silent, purposeful movement that sent shudders through her.

'Like this,' he said.

He caught her against him, his mouth taking hers in a kiss that gave no quarter. Dimly, Lauren realised that it was a signal of dominant masculinity, and she gloried in it, demanding as much from him as he asked from her, her eager body thrumming with need.

He kissed her as though she was the only woman he'd ever wanted, as though they shared infinitely more than this transitory passion, this time out of time in the empty blue reaches of the Pacific.

Shuddering, she opened her mouth to his, and relished the wild kick of passion inside her—and the fierce hardness of his body against hers.

'When I first saw you,' he said, reluctantly giving her air, 'I wanted you.' That faint trace of accent flavoured each word, intriguing and different.

'Mmm,' she murmured. 'You looked like a pirate. A very sexy pirate.'

His heavy eyelids almost covered his eyes, but she could see a gleam of laughter in their golden depths. 'You have a thing for pirates?'

'Stubble suits some people,' she said demurely, nipping her way along his jawbone.

He laughed again, deep and low and triumphant, and kissed the spot where her neck joined her shoulders, and then the warm swell of her breasts above her sarong. Pleasure raced through her in a dizzying flood; as he deftly untied the knot she knew that nothing in her previous life had prepared her for the ardent, honeyed recklessness of making love with Guy.

When the sarong fell away, he froze. Lauren gazed into his stunned face, and her heart tumbled into freefall. She hadn't known a man could look like that—a mixture of conqueror and supplicant, eyes glittering in a darkly drawn face while he gazed at the slender white curves and lines of her body.

And then he lifted his head, and there was no supplication in his expression now—he was all conqueror. Her breath locked deliciously in her chest when he cupped a small, high breast, tanned fingers shaping the pale curves with erotic confidence as his thumb brushed the tight pink bud at the centre, slowly, back and forth, back and forth, until she moaned deep in her throat.

Needles of pure desire ran along her nerves; she couldn't speak, couldn't tell him that he was killing her with sensation. Even her breath died when he bent his head and kissed the nipple his thumb had tantalised. Carnal sensation sparked an inferno inside her when the tight little nub peaked in a silent, evocative plea for more.

He gave it to her, his dark head drawing close. Lauren swallowed, and when he drew the nipple into his mouth her knees buckled.

Guy caught her before she fell, lifting her into his arms and stepping over the fallen sarong to carry her across to the bed. As her feet touched the floor, his free hand jerked aside the bright quilted coverlet and he put her down gently on her back.

'Are you sure?' he asked deeply, his gaze caressing her body, exposed now for his delight with only a scrap of cotton hiding her most secret parts.

They had so little time, Lauren thought desperately. Soon she'd be leaving for New Zealand.

And Guy? He'd go back to Sant'Rosa, and she had no right to ask him to stay away.

A smile trembled along her lips. 'Utterly sure,' she said like a vow.

Guy stood very still, then said, 'So am I,' and without haste he shrugged out of his shirt.

Her pulses drummed faster as she feasted her eyes on the clean, perfect symmetry of his body. But when he stood naked before her, her breath locked in her throat. He was, she realised on a note of primitive panic, big all over, and it had been a long time since she'd done this...

'Relax,' he said softly, and ran a deliberate forefinger from the centre of her breast to the soft, warm nest between her thighs. 'I won't hurt you.'

The path of that finger burned like a streak of fire, and her confidence returned in a rush. Her first glance had told her that he was an experienced lover. 'I know.'

Solemnly she watched the play of powerful muscles beneath his sleek bronze skin as he untied the mosquito netting so that it fell around the bed in a billow of white, shutting them off from the rest of the world.

Then he came down beside her, dark to her light, sun to her moon, strength to her grace.

CHAPTER FIVE

LAUREN had expected a slow, sophisticated wooing. Perhaps Guy had planned that, but when she smoothed her hand over his shoulder and down the flexible line of his spine, her fingers tracing out the vertebrae beneath the hot skin, he muttered a word she couldn't discern. And followed it with another devouring kiss that set her afire with heady, primal intoxication.

A ferocious intensity wiped away the last pathetic shreds of her self-control. When she gasped and arched beneath him, her hips grinding into his, he took an importunate, demanding nipple into his mouth and suckled strongly.

Delicious arrows blazed through her body; groaning, she tightened her fingers around his head, holding him close to her breast while the craving intensified, burning hotter and hotter until she thought she might die of need.

'Now,' she muttered. 'Now, for heaven's sake… Guy, please—'

He kissed her again, and a second later he was buried to the hilt in her, his big body so rigid she thought he might not be able to control himself any longer.

But he dragged a quick, impeded breath into his lungs, and slowly, deliciously eased out of the slick passage until she gasped his name again, and once more her hips jerked in involuntary provocation.

On a harsh, feral sound, he thrust even deeper inside her, and she met the powerful rhythm and matched it until every thought fled her brain, lost in the sensual tidal wave of Guy's mastery.

It was like drowning in rapture, and for a sudden moment she fought it, wondering where it would lead, what it would take from her.

'Relax,' he said, the words purring roughly into her ear. 'Let go, Lauren—it won't hurt. It can't hurt.'

Yes, it can, she thought wildly, her head tossing back and forth on the pillow, but it was too late. She could no more resist this blatant bewitchment of her senses than she could push him off; she had never before felt so much a woman, so much herself, as she did when Guy made love to her.

Anyway, she couldn't speak. The pleasure that had been threatening her since her first sight of him boosted her into some stratosphere of sensation. Her lashes flew up and she stared into his face. Lean and dark, every arrogant bone prominent, eyes glittering like the heart of the sun, he looked like a corsair intent on plunder.

And she was it, and she wanted it as much as he did. Lauren abandoned every last inhibition and surrendered to passion, rocking herself against him and tightening her inner muscles in an ancient, provocative rhythm every time he pushed into her.

She saw the moment his control cracked and shattered, registered the split-second of understanding in his aristocratic face, and then the torrent of ecstasy rolled over and through her in waves from the centre of her body.

Savage, merciless, exquisitely arousing, they hurled her into an alternate universe where all she saw was the golden gleam of Guy's eyes and all she felt was an ineffable rapture that lasted too long and not long enough, where its slow fading was at once a tragedy and a glory.

And then Guy followed her into that secret, bewildering place, a low, hoarse sound torn from his throat as he fought for that peak, his beautiful body like steel against her and in her.

As the savage physical longing ebbed into sweet sorrow, Lauren linked her arms around his neck and pulled his head down to kiss him. Yielding to her conviction that he needed her had brought her wild ecstasy, but she'd chosen to break through an invisible barrier into another world where invisible chains linked her to him.

How would she ever forget him?

Mouth still holding hers captive, Guy rolled onto his back, scooping her with him so that she was lying on him.

When they could both breathe again, both speak, he asked, 'When are you leaving Valanu?'

Her heart wept, but she answered steadily, 'When funds come through for a plane ticket.'

'I'm returning to Sant'Rosa three days from now,' he said. 'Would you like to spend those days with me?'

Lauren lifted her head to stare into his eyes; she saw the pupils dilate, and the fracture in her heart widened as she pulled back. Although the residual heat of passion still smouldered in the golden depths, she realised that once she left Valanu she'd never see Guy again. At least, she thought painfully, he made no promises, offered no inducements. 'Here?'

'A little further along the coast.'

'On a desert island?' she asked, putting off the moment of decision.

His smile was a sensual challenge. 'Deserted,' he said. 'Not exactly an island.'

Although she hesitated, she knew what answer she'd give him. 'Yes. But I'll have to ring my parents and tell them what's happening.'

He kissed her collar-bone. 'Everything?' he asked wickedly.

And although it hurt, she smiled. 'Not everything,' she admitted, and yawned.

'You can tell them when we get there.'

'You've got a telephone on your deserted not-island?'

He tucked her against his shoulder. 'Yes. Now, go to sleep. We'll leave at dawn tomorrow morning.'

But he woke her once more, and towards dawn she woke him, and both times they made love with slow, sweet passion that culminated in white-hot savagery, leaving them sensually replete.

Sputtering across the lagoon in a banana boat, Lauren turned to look at Guy. Something about his stance, his expression as he frowned into the sun and steered, sent a shiver across her nerve ends. Dismissing the momentary unease, she said lightly, 'Where did you learn to run a departure like a military exercise?'

The canoe met the oncoming wave a little clumsily, splashing a sparkling cascade of water over the bow. 'I did army training for a couple of years,' he said. 'It's a tradition in my family. Look, can you see the frigate birds?' He pointed to a pair of long-tailed birds that swooped above the lagoon.

In other words, she thought bleakly, do not go there, Lauren.

That morning she'd woken in his arms, and for a few seconds she'd allowed herself to feel at home there—until common sense took over, reminding her that Guy belonged in some way to Sant'Rosa, and she was a rising executive in her half-brother's large organisation. Apart from the passion that blazed between them, they just didn't connect—something Guy clearly understood, and something she had to accept.

Although the house he took her to sprawled alone beneath the coconut palms lining another white beach, there was nothing primitive about it. 'Does this lovely place belong to you?' she asked after she'd rung her parents using the latest in communications technology.

'No. The resort,' Guy told her. 'The owner wanted to build a dozen or so along the lagoon, but his plans fell through. Do you like it?'

She gazed around the open, airy room, decorated in the blue of the lagoon, the soft green of the palm leaves and the white of the sand, and smiled a little ironically. Of course a buccaneer wouldn't have a home.

'It's beautiful,' she said, her voice dying as he kissed her.

During the next few days Lauren learned how lost in desire she could become; this new capacity for sensation both overwhelmed and scared her. But because these precious days were all that she'd have of Guy, she surrendered to erotic fantasy—and the arms and body of a man who set himself to satisfy appetites she hadn't known existed.

Time enough to consider the implications when she returned to the workaday world.

He was the perfect lover—intelligent, intriguing, and he could cook. He made her laugh and he talked about anything she wanted to discuss, although by mutual consent neither spoke of their ordinary lives.

And he seemed to know by instinct when she wanted tenderness, when she wanted to walk on the wild side, and when she wanted to sleep. She soon lost any inhibitions about swimming naked in water as warm as her blood, walking back to the house over sand like powdered sugar to shower with him in the huge bathroom.

Sun-warmed, star-silvered, threaded with passion, the days and nights slid through her fingers like pearls on a silken cord, perfect, irretrievable, until at last it was the morning they were due back in Valanu. Just before they left Lauren spoke to her parents again.

Guy left her to check that everything was ready, coming back in the brightening light to hear her say, 'I thought I might come straight back home instead of going on to New Zealand.'

He'd heard her voice in so many moods—sultry, playful, sophisticated, determined, and the way he liked best, shaken by craving—but never the warmly affectionate tone she used for her parents.

So? he thought restlessly.

She listened, then said, 'Well—are you sure?'

A long silence followed, during which her soft mouth tilted at the corners in a smile she'd never bestowed on him. He watched a graceful hand trace a pattern on the table and responded to the familiar heaviness in his loins with tight anger. He didn't want to feel like this. They had made love so many times he'd lost count; with Lauren he was insatiable and her response was equally reckless, but she had been careful to avoid any reference to the future.

Perhaps she was that rare thing, a woman who treated her lovers with affection, then let them go without any emotional strings.

Until that moment he'd deliberately pushed the shadow of Marc Corbett to the furthest reaches of his mind, but now a jagged pang of jealousy, barbaric in its intensity, thrust through his iron control. Guy had always considered himself a sophisticated man, one who didn't expect anything more from his lovers than he was prepared to give them—affection, respect and good sex.

Yet the thought of Lauren going from his bed to another man's summoned a primitive possessiveness that infuriated him.

'Well, all right,' she said cheerfully into the telephone. 'I'm leaving today, but I have a few hours' stopover in Fiji so I won't get to New Zealand until late. I'll spend the night at an airport hotel in Auckland and fly up to the Bay of Islands tomorrow morning.'

She listened again, then laughed. 'Fusspot. Yes, I'll ring you as soon as I get to Marc's house. Goodbye.' She put the telephone down.

A fierce, elemental anger almost consumed Guy; unlike his normal coldly disciplined response to provocation, this hot outrage seethed under such pressure that it took his entire stock of will-power to restrain it.

'Everything under control?' It was all he could trust himself to say, and even then his voice sounded guttural and aggressive.

Grey eyes wary, she looked up. Clearly, she hadn't heard him come in. 'Yes, thank you. I wondered if I should go home to reassure them that their darling daughter is safe and healthy, but my father wouldn't hear of it.'

Guy wrestled his simmering rage into enough of a strait-jacket to say curtly, 'A thoughtful father.'

So she was going to Marc Corbett's house. It could mean nothing more than that they were on good terms even though their relationship had ended. It wasn't so unusual; he prided himself on staying good friends with his previous lovers. He'd have offered a holiday house to any of them.

But it might also mean that the time they'd spent together meant nothing more to her than an exotic interlude.

He tried for a mental shrug, wondering coldly why his usual practical logic had abandoned him. So what? They'd made no commitment; Lauren might be every man's dream lover, but their idyll was over. She could go wherever she wanted, sleep with whomever she wanted. And so could he.

Her tone deepened. 'My father's a darling.' She joined him on the tiled terrace outside the airy sitting room and said carefully, 'Guy, it's been magic. Thank you so much.'

'You sound like a small child at the end of a party,' he said, exasperated by the rasping undertone in his voice.

Her face went still. Without moving she met his eyes, her own now as opaque as burnished silver, but her withdrawal hit him, palpable as a blow.

Steadily she said, 'Probably because that's what I feel like. It's been a lovely, lovely party, but like all good times, it's come to an end.'

Hiding his astonishing anger with the disciplined control he'd fought to acquire, Guy relaxed hands that were curling into fists by his sides. 'You'd better give me an address so I can contact you if I need to.'

At first he thought she was going to refuse, but she nodded and reached into her bag for a small notebook. He watched her write down the address, tear the page out and hand it over. 'I'll be there for three weeks,' she told him, that seamless poise firmly in place.

Guy wanted to smash it into splinters. Get a grip, he

told himself roughly. A few days making love to a woman gave you no claims to her.

'Right, we'd better go,' he said, and picked up the bags.

They got back to Valanu not too long before her plane was due to leave. As the banana boat sputtered across the brilliant blues of the lagoon, Lauren gazed around, pretending that nothing had changed, that Guy wasn't steering with an expression of such concentrated authority it shut her out as effectively as a barred door.

A car was waiting at the docks; Guy must have organised it. He walked her towards it, and as the driver slung her bag into the boot she held out her hand in farewell and said steadily, 'Goodbye. Thank you for everything.'

Equally formal, his golden eyes dark and unreadable in his handsome face, he bowed over her hand. But there was nothing formal about the way he lifted it to his mouth; his kiss burned against her skin like a brand, quickening her heart and tightening inner muscles accustomed now to enclosing him in their subtle grip.

'It was,' he said with silken distinctness, 'my complete and utter pleasure.'

Colour scorched along her cheekbones; she looked away, blinking at the figure of a man in the distance. 'Mine too,' she said uncertainly.

He held open the door and she slid into the back of the car. It drew away and she didn't look back; she didn't even notice the man who stared into the vehicle as it passed him, then straightened to examine Guy, a big figure striding into the distance.

During the flight to Sant'Rosa's capital and then on to Fiji, she fought a savage, unrelenting emptiness, refusing food and anything to drink except water and fruit juice. Once aboard the big jet for New Zealand, she watched the jewel that was Fiji's main island drop away from beneath the plane's wings and forced herself to eat something that tasted like a mixture of plastic and sawdust in her mouth.

Afterwards she saw the sun go down in a splendour of blood-red and scarlet, and blamed the sight for eyes that felt heavy and dry, as though if she relaxed they might sting with tears.

Stop that right now, she told herself roundly. You knew right from the start that once you left you'd never see Guy again. You knew, and you accepted it—you can't renege on the deal now.

She was not in love with Guy Bagaton.

But halfway to New Zealand she finally accepted something she'd been refusing to acknowledge. She had done the exact same thing as her mother—without considering anything other than her own desires, she'd embarked on a wild, defiant, unrestrained affair with a man she didn't know.

At least, she thought tiredly, she wasn't married, as her mother had been. And there would be no pregnancy—Guy had seen to that. A hollow sadness took her by surprise, and was hastily banished.

But Isabel Porter had known more about her lover than Lauren knew about hers. The genetic father Lauren shared with Marc Corbett had been a businessman of note, a lover of beautiful women and a rampantly unfaithful husband notorious for his affairs. Although her mother had known he was married—and been married herself—she'd been unable to resist his powerful magnetism.

Just like me, Lauren thought, hands tensely locking together in her lap. I am truly my mother's daughter.

And my father's!

Well, her *genetic* father's. Her *true* father was Hugh Porter, who discovered that the daughter he had considered his own was the result of his wife's adultery only when Lauren was in her early twenties. As he was already fighting heart disease, the shock had almost killed him, but he had forgiven Isabel and reassured Lauren of a love that had never faltered.

Her mouth setting into a straight line, she steered her thoughts away from that period. Guy could be a planter of some sort; rice, or indigo or copra—whatever planters produced on tropical islands. He could be a scout for one of the forestry companies that were buying tropical hardwoods; he'd been scathing enough about the *sali* nut scheme to make this possible.

Half-pirate, half-warrior, he lived on an island marooned in the endless blue waves of the Pacific Ocean. Apart from sharing a blazing sexual attraction, they had nothing in common. She lived and worked in London. She loved her career, and her favourite city was Paris— about as different from the steamy heat of Sant'Rosa as any place could be.

Her lips formed the words *nothing in common* as they echoed in her mind with cold resonance. A giant fist squeezed her heart into a painful knot.

Of course she had to repay the money he'd lent her, but that wouldn't need personal contact. She didn't have his address, but she'd soon find one; everyone was traceable on the Internet. And even if he wasn't, any letter addressed to him in Sant'Rosa would find its way to him. Everyone there seemed to know him.

And he had her address…

For the rest of the journey to New Zealand she stared

unseeingly ahead while her treacherous mind replayed images of the time she'd spent in Guy's arms.

Once she got to Marc's house in New Zealand she'd be fine. She'd recover from this inconvenient and heady rush of blood to the loins, and be her normal self again.

Well, she thought drearily, I now know what happens when you hit the tropics—madness.

Lauren stroked the elderly golden retriever's insistent head.

'No, Fancy,' she said patiently, 'I don't want to go for a walk along the beach, and no, I don't want to row you around to Cabbage Tree Bay, and no, I don't want to climb the hill either. Nor do I want to throw your ball or feed you treats.'

All I want to do, she finished silently, is lie here in the sun and mourn a man I won't see again.

Tail wagging, Fancy sighed, gave her a forgiving lick on the fingers, and flopped down in the sun beside the lounger. Lauren's eyes narrowed against the glare as she gazed out across the bay; although this was a distant reach of the huge Pacific Ocean, it was much cooler and more green than the warm tropical seas surrounding Valanu and Sant'Rosa.

'But just as beautiful,' she said sternly.

Fancy's tail thumped agreement. Now and forever, Lauren knew, she'd measure every island against Valanu, where Guy had taught her the exquisite pleasures of sex.

For long forbidden minutes she lay still and remembered—as she'd been remembering for the past two days. Two days and four hours, actually. At least, she thought drearily, she wasn't counting the minutes…

Fancy sat up, ears pricked and alert as she stared into the sky.

'What is it, girl?' But Lauren too had heard it by now—a helicopter, coming fast and low.

Her half-brother, Marc? No, he and Paige were still enjoying a second honeymoon in the Seychelles, having left their adorable twin daughters with Marc's doting mother in Paris.

Some secret instinct shortened Lauren's breath. Telling herself not to be an idiot, she sprinted inside to change her brief shorts and top for linen trousers and a silk shirt.

'Just in case,' she murmured, and gave a dreary little laugh. Of course it wouldn't be Guy.

And if by some miracle it was Guy, she'd send him away. Even if he wanted her to, she couldn't see herself spending the rest of her life on a tropical island.

'Oh, you idiot,' she muttered, hastily masking her face with a discreet film of cosmetics. 'When did you start thinking in terms of the rest of your life? He certainly wasn't considering permanence.'

Combing her hair into place, she wondered what on earth had happened to her normally disciplined brain.

'You let yourself be ambushed by temptation. You blatantly let him know you were available, and you didn't put up even a minor objection when he carried you off for days of hot sex and wild passion,' she muttered.

OK, so other people did things like that all the time, but she'd been utterly irresponsible. She should have fled to New Zealand the minute he handed over her passport on Valanu.

Even then, it was too late. That hasty fake marriage conducted under gunfire was just the sort of human-

interest story a journalist would love. To save her
mother humiliation and her father the stress that wors-
ened his precarious health, she and Marc had always
been careful not to attract attention to their relationship.

Frowning, she slid on small gold earrings as the
chopper eased down towards the pad behind the house.

She'd been lucky because it didn't seem that her
recklessness had compromised the old, hidden scandal
of her conception. Surely, if any journalist had got a
sniff of her time with Guy—or of that fake marriage—
it would have turned up in the papers by now. They'd
been having a great time with the heroic, unknown
'Englishman' who'd fought side by side with the
Sant'Rosan forces.

A knock on the door announced the housekeeper.
'Lauren, it's a Mr Bagaton,' she said, looking both in-
trigued and slightly put out. 'He insists on seeing you.'

Lauren's stomach clenched, a chaotic surge of joy
wiping everything but anticipation from her mind.
Trying hard not to beam, she said, 'Thanks, Mrs Oliver.
I know him.'

He was waiting in the morning room, completely relaxed in casual trousers that clung to his long, muscular
legs. The rolled sleeves of his shirt revealed tanned fore-
arms. He had shaved.

Yet there was nothing casual in the way he watched
her come across the room; narrowed, intent eyes in an
impassive face examined her as though she was some
rare specimen he'd been searching a lifetime for.

Sensation slammed through her, hot and unashamedly
primeval.

This was a different man from the one on Sant'Rosa,
the beachcomber, the man of action, the lover. He was
harder, his control an icy cloak around him, and there

was something about his dark gaze that sent tremors scudding the length of her spine.

Yet her body had sprung to life at the first glimpse of him; that consuming hunger surged through every cell, ran molten along her nerves, fired synapses all through her body until she burned with elemental urgency.

She'd never thought to meet anyone to match her half-brother, Marc, yet now another man stood in his house clothed in the same ruthless authority, exerting the same effortless dominance.

Calling on every shred of restraint, she said, 'Good morning, Guy. This is an unexpected pleasure.'

Her composed, measured greeting brought a swift, taunting smile. Before she realised what he intended he covered the distance between them in three long strides and dropped a stinging kiss on her startled mouth, before stepping back. 'I'm glad it's a pleasure.'

'Of course,' she said, hiding the uncertainty in her tone with a quick, abrupt delivery. 'What brings you here?'

'You look pale—are you all right?'

'I'm fine.' Oh, *fine* was such an inadequate word! She was terrified at how alive she felt now, reborn by his presence.

Still frowning, he said, 'Sit down.'

An icy bubble suddenly expanded beneath her ribs. She searched his face, but the hard angles and planes revealed nothing. 'Why?'

'I'm not a bearer of good news.'

Shaking her head, she unconsciously stiffened her shoulders. 'Tell me.'

But it wasn't until another rapid, unsparing survey apparently reassured him she had the stamina to deal with what he had to say that he told her bluntly, 'The marriage we contracted in Sant'Rosa might be legal.'

CHAPTER SIX

'IT'S legal?' Ashen-faced, Lauren stared at him.

'According to my lawyer we could be on shaky ground if we assume it's not binding.' He spoke levelly, no emotions showing in either tone or expression.

Rallying, she exploded, 'But there was no licence, no identification—nothing but the form that—that—'

'Josef,' Guy supplied helpfully.

'That Josef had with him.' She unclenched the fists at her sides. 'It cannot possibly be legal.'

Guy's broad shoulders lifted in a negligent shrug. 'On Sant'Rosa, it seems, the ceremony and Josef's form might be enough.'

Numbly Lauren walked across to the window, staring out at the picture-perfect garden, lushly subtropical, familiar and safe. The dog, Fancy, wandered across the lawn and spread herself out on the terrace in the sun, yawning prodigiously before curling up for another of her interminable naps.

Panic hollowed out her stomach, brought her brain skidding to a halt. *Married to Guy Bagaton?*

'No,' she said starkly. 'I won't accept it.'

'Accepting it or not isn't going to make a blind bit of difference,' Guy stated with brutal frankness. 'And it's not certain; my solicitors are working on it. I thought you should know so that you can be prepared.'

'Thank you.' She took a deep breath and forced her brain into action.

Even if the marriage was valid, it would only be a

nuisance. It would take time and money she couldn't afford to sort out, but that was all. That had to be all; she couldn't let memories of the time they'd spent together affect her—they certainly weren't affecting him.

But if a journalist got to hear about it, there was a chance that someone might dig deeper to discover the secret at the heart of her life. She'd cope—but her parents had to be protected.

Taking a deep breath, she asked, 'When will you know?'.

'Things are still confused in Sant'Rosa, but my solicitor is confident that he'll get an answer within two weeks. I shall, of course, let you know immediately.'

She nodded stiffly. 'Thank you,' she said again.

Eyes narrowed golden slivers beneath heavy eyelids, Guy scrutinised her face. 'However, if this gets out you may find journalists contacting you to ask about your escape from Sant'Rosa.'

Lauren's stomach dropped. Before she could stop herself, she said, 'Oh, God no! The last thing I want is the media poking around in my life!'

Black brows lifting, he scanned her like a predator assessing prey, yet his voice was idly enquiring when he asked, 'Any particular reason?'

Careful, she cautioned herself. 'Just an innate dislike of figuring in headlines.'

He observed casually, 'Which is why I warned you. Don't answer the phone—tell the housekeeper to say you're not here.'

Logic kicked in just in time to stop her from panicking. 'But surely public interest in a small war on a tiny island nation is already waning? I noticed there wasn't much in this morning's paper.' She added with a smile that was a bit lopsided, 'I'm sure they'd like to discover the identity of "the mysterious Englishman" who fought for the Sant'Rosans, although that must be stale news now too.'

'Unfortunately some fools tried to shoot down a plane leaving the airport,' he said bluntly. 'It's stirred up the whole hornet's nest again.'

Lauren bit her lip. 'I can't imagine Josef will tell anyone what happened.'

'It's unlikely,' he agreed, angular features hard and determined, 'but there were other people in the terminal building that night.'

'They wouldn't have seen anything,' she said evenly, thoughts milling uselessly around in her mind. Trying to convince herself, she added, 'And the journalists will be war correspondents. Surely they won't be interested.'

'A reporter is always a reporter. Curiosity is their trade.' When she stayed silent he went on, 'It's not exactly a death sentence if you appear in a headline or two.'

His choice of words startled her, but she told herself not to overreact. Even if someone found out about the marriage ceremony, it didn't mean that they'd pry any deeper into her life. Even if they did—

'If you're worried about anyone discovering that we spent several days together on Valanu—'

'No,' she said too quickly. 'Well, I'd sooner it didn't star in a media frenzy, of course, but I'm sure they won't be interested in that.'

Resisting a gaze that frightened her with its probing intelligence, she finished on what she fervently hoped was a throwaway note, 'Of course you'll look even more of a hero than you already are.' She indicated a newspaper on the table.

Ignoring it, he shrugged. 'It means nothing.'

That maddening flash of memory resurfaced, only to vanish, leaving her to stare into the face of a stranger— a stranger she knew more intimately than any other man.

'I know,' she said stiffly. 'It's just that I value my privacy.'

'As do we all.' He looked around the elegant, civilised room and said, 'This house is a far cry from Valanu. Are you going to show me the beach?'

Baffled and hurt by the whip-flick of contempt in his words, she said, 'Yes, of course.'

They went out into the mellow autumn sunlight, Fancy joining them with a frisk of her head. Guy crouched down to stroke the golden head with a skill that indicated familiarity with dogs.

Fancy, of course, adored him, wriggling with delight when he scratched in exactly the right place behind her ears. Well, the dog was female, Lauren thought with a queer twist in her heart. Acquaintance made, he stood up in a lithe movement, tall and strong against the green of the garden, and looked around him with an expressionless face.

Lauren scanned the bold, autocratic bone structure, skin tingling as though she'd brushed up against an electric fence. 'If we are married—if the ceremony was legal—what can we do?'

'Annulment on the grounds of non-consummation being out of the question,' he said curtly, 'I presume it will mean divorce.'

A pang of—bitterness?—ripped through her. Trying to regain some sense of control, she dragged in a deep breath and led the way down to the beach. She bent sideways to take off her sandals and dropped them on the grassy bank beneath one of the huge pohutukawa trees. 'Surely it will be invalid everywhere but Sant'Rosa?'

Despising the pleading note in her voice, she clamped her mouth on more words. When Guy didn't answer she swung around to face him.

He said coolly, 'A marriage contracted legally in one country is usually legal in any other, unless it's polygamous. Even underage marriages are not necessarily invalid.'

Lauren concentrated on relaxing her taut muscles as she walked beside him along the sand, pleasantly warm beneath the soles of her feet. A gull soared up in front of them with a shriek that sounded too much like derisive laughter.

'Thanks for warning me,' she said slowly.

Fancy pushed into her, offering comfort for an emotion she'd never understand—one even Lauren didn't recognise.

Guy's face was a handsome mask over his thoughts. 'If anyone contacts you, simply refuse to comment.' He waited before adding with exquisite suavity, 'You needn't, of course, be concerned that I plan to claim any marital rights.'

Colour scorched along her cheekbones. 'I'm not,' she said shortly. 'Why didn't Josef tell us it might be valid?'

Guy's mouth thinned. 'If you remember, he warned us that it might be valid only on Sant'Rosa. But what else was he to do? He's a good bureaucrat—even with his world falling to pieces around him, he wouldn't send you to another country without papers.'

Lauren's teeth savaged her lower lip for a second. Faced with the horror of war, Josef had done what he could to save her from a similar fate.

She said on a sigh, 'If you wanted to make me feel like a heel, you've succeeded. Is he all right?'

'As all right as a man can be who has lost his oldest son,' he said brusquely.

Lauren's eyes filled with sudden tears. 'I'm sorry,' she said again, groping for a handkerchief to wipe her eyes and blow her nose. 'Against that, I haven't got much to complain about.'

'Not a lot.' His tone was so dry it could have soaked up a minor lake or two. 'It's not a disaster, Lauren; inconvenient, certainly, and with the prospect of some rather fulsome and irritating publicity if it gets out, but nothing to panic about.'

Head held high, Lauren said, 'Of course. But I don't consider myself married to you!'

'That,' he said calmly, 'is entirely mutual. On reflection, our charming idyll on Valanu was rash, but hindsight is always wiser than foresight.' He turned and examined the house, a sprawling white place mellow with many years of love and care. 'If the ceremony turns out to be legal, I'll contact you so that we can apply to whatever court has the power to have the marriage dissolved.'

'Thank you,' she said automatically.

Still with his gaze on the house, he said, 'You have a very indulgent employer. Does he allow all his executives to take their holidays in his private hideaway?'

How did he know that Marc was her employer?

Then she realised what he was implying.

Cool distaste coloured her tone. 'You'll have to ask him that.'

'I assume your fear of the media is in case your lover hears about your indiscretion on Valanu,' he said, his pleasant tone failing to hide the steely edge in the words.

'What?'

He said contemptuously, 'Don't lie to me. I know you are his mistress, since even before he married his lovely New Zealander.'

One of the first things Marc taught her was that losing her temper put her at an immediate disadvantage. With his advice in mind, Lauren had kept her cool when facing down unfriendly meetings, rejecting sexual harassment and dealing with carpet sellers in Middle Eastern markets.

Pain clawed her so sharply that she lost control. 'My life is none of your business,' she said in a voice that should have turned the ground beneath them to permafrost.

Black brows climbed just enough to indicate Guy's total and scornful disbelief. 'When you invited me into your bed and your arms, it became my business,' he said silkily.

Stabbed by a searing mixture of anguish and outrage, she said thinly, 'That was an—an aberration.'

He laughed. 'A very pleasurable one for me,' he drawled.

'I am not Marc Corbett's mistress,' she ground out.

'It is an old-fashioned term, I agree. Do you prefer lover?'

Her lips tightened. 'Neither.' Trying to regain control of the situation, she went on, 'Before I decide what to do, I'll consult my solicitor. He might be able to find out something yours hasn't.'

Guy stopped and looked down at her, narrowed golden eyes uncompromising in the stark framework of his face. 'Get this straight,' he said flatly. '*You* don't decide—we're in this together.'

Her mouth dried. 'I didn't mean that I'd make a unilateral decision.'

After a pause he said abruptly, 'Tell me about your relationship with Marc Corbett.'

Guy watched the familiar blankness shut down her expression. When her tongue stole out to wet her lips, he had to rein in the lash of desire that cut through him.

She said quietly, 'I don't know whether I can trust you.'

Cold fury stirred beneath the desire. 'I can't, of course, force your confidence.'

She glanced up, pale eyes glinting and intelligent. After a long moment she said abruptly, 'He saved my life.'

Astonishment replaced his anger. Whatever he'd expected to hear, it wasn't that. 'How?'

Muscles moved beneath the silken skin of her throat as she swallowed. 'Just after I graduated from university I developed leukaemia.'

His blood ran cold. 'Go on.'

'I needed a bone marrow transplant, but they couldn't find one to suit.' She spoke dispassionately, as though it had happened to some other woman. 'In the end we discovered that Marc was a perfect match. If he hadn't been, I'd have died.'

The ugly clutch of fear fading, Guy said slowly, 'I see.' It was outrageous, unbelievable that this lovely, vital woman had been threatened by death.

Lauren stopped to pick up a shell. Keeping her gaze on its pearly sheen and intricate spirals, she said, 'After that, I hero-worshipped him a bit.'

'I can understand that.' The crispness of his tone hid, he hoped, the questions seething through his mind.

How had her doctors found that Marc Corbett was a bone marrow match? Common sense told him that the man had probably enrolled on the worldwide register— but why? And surely donors' names were kept secret?

Lauren looked at him with eyes so translucent it seemed impossible for her to hide a thought. 'He told me that when I got better he'd give me a job if I wanted one and if I was suitable; of course I was delighted, and when I got the all-clear I fronted up. I had to go through the same process as anyone else, but I got in, and ever since then we've had a sort of—well, closeness. I try not to impose on it, but he's a darling, and so is his wife, Paige.'

Guy's mouth curved in an ironic smile. He liked Marc Corbett and respected him, but *darling* wasn't a word he'd have used to describe the man.

Once again she lifted limpid eyes to his. Her voice rang true, she was looking him straight in the face, but instincts honed in the cutthroat world he'd made his own told him she was lying. Or at the very least, only revealing part of the truth.

Coldly, clinically, he decided that if her story was a front for an affair, it had the advantage of originality. Even if it was true, she could still be Marc Corbett's lover.

As for her obvious affection for Paige Corbett, it wouldn't be the first—or the last—time a woman had an ongoing relationship with the husband of a friend.

Lauren wondered uneasily what was going on behind those fabulous features, gilded by sunlight. Did he believe her? And had it been enough to satisfy him?

She found herself wishing she could trust him with

the whole truth. If it had just been herself she might have, but in the end it wasn't her secret.

She said brightly, 'It's an old story, and not one I'd like to get around. Some people say that if you save someone's life you're responsible for them forever afterwards; I'd hate people to believe Marc gave me a job because of some quirk of genetic good fortune.'

'I can understand that,' Guy said with a smile that blended irony with a hint of self-derision.

Sunlight conjured a shimmer of mahogany fire from his black hair. He dragged out a wallet from his pocket, scribbled something on a page of a small diary, and tore it out to hand to her. 'In case you need me,' he said.

Their fingers touched, and Lauren's heart jumped.

'And just to remind you how it was with us—' he said through his teeth, and covered the three paces that separated them, drawing her into his arms.

Every nerve speared by forbidden delight, Lauren froze. He looked down into her face, his own angrily intent. 'No, you haven't forgotten,' he said in a raw voice.

And then he kissed her eyelids closed, his breath warm on her skin.

Pierced by erotic poignancy, Lauren's defences crumbled into sand. This was what she'd been waiting for— this sense of rightness, of completeness...

His lips crushed hers in a kiss that obliterated all sense of time and space. Helplessly she melted into his arms and gave him everything he asked for, responding with feverish passion to his sensuous onslaught.

But although she wanted nothing more than to let this go on to its inevitable conclusion, she finally fought free of the consuming hunger to shake her head and drag her mouth from his, gasping hoarsely, 'No!'

A fierce, possessive gleam fired his eyes. 'But you were saying yes a moment ago.'

Even then she hovered on the brink of surrender until hard common sense forced its way through the mists of desire.

'No,' she repeated quietly, uncompromisingly, because she knew that she'd never be safe, that the only way to stop herself from falling headlong into infatuation was to end it now.

But oh, it was hard to say, with his strength and his heat seducing her, with the sexy, evocative aroma of his skin scrambling her brain, and his taste on her lips, in her mouth—when every cell in her body screamed for the release only he could give her.

His mouth hardened. 'Why?'

'Because I don't want this.' The lie hurt, and it hurt more that he knew it was a lie. 'I find you very attractive,' she hurried on, surprised at the clarity of each word, 'but the idea of being married to you—if that's what I am—is ridiculous. And I certainly don't want an affair with you.'

She invested the final word with a flick of scorn, and saw it register on his face. He smiled, and as she shivered he freed her and stepped back.

'Really?' he said politely. 'I can think of plenty of words to describe such a marriage, but ridiculous doesn't come to mind. As for the affair— I thought we'd already had it.'

'We spent a few days together,' she corrected, gripped by intolerable anguish. Yet she had to send him out of her life. 'I'm sorry, but a tropical fling is not expected to last beyond the tropics. I'll always be grateful to you for saving my life, because I suspect that's what you did.'

'Stop right there,' he advised with an inflection so deadly it chilled her into temporary paralysis. 'If you're telling me that you slept with me out of gratitude, I'll just have to show you that you're wrong. We made love because we wanted each other.'

'Of course I did—we did!' She struggled to clear her mind. 'You know very well that I—that we—that it was mutual.' She stopped and dragged in a jerky breath before finishing defiantly, 'But it's over.'

For a charged moment he surveyed her, his beautiful mouth hard against the chiselled angles of his face. Finally he drawled, 'Then there's nothing more to say,' and turned away. 'Goodbye, Lauren.'

Aching with a bleak sense of loss and pain, she watched him stride towards the thick row of trees that hid the helicopter pad. Fate and war had shackled them together until they could get free of this marriage.

Whatever she felt for Guy Bagaton couldn't possibly be love; that involved much more than gratitude and great sex.

Only a loser would love a man who thought she was another man's mistress, and she wasn't a loser. She didn't even know him.

Not really.

The sound of the helicopter's rotor blades drove her to shelter beneath the overhanging branches of one of the great trees bordering the champagne curve of the beach. As she listened to the machine carry Guy away from her, she found herself thinking of all the ways she did know him...

Perhaps when people had forgotten about the war in Sant'Rosa, it might be safe to see him again. Without all this other baggage cluttering up their relationship, they could perhaps meet as ordinary people.

No. She'd sent him away.

And she'd do it again. When she'd asked her mother why, of all the people in the world, Marc's bone marrow matched hers, Isabel's admission of adultery had been shattering enough, but what had appalled her was her mother's response when Lauren began to ask if her father knew.

After the first two tentative words her mother had interrupted fiercely, 'He does now. Don't ever speak to him about it. The stress could kill him.'

Lauren didn't know how her parents had worked through this rough patch, but their love had held them together through the trauma.

When the steady thump-thump-thump of the rotors had died away, she went back inside and rang London.

'How's Dad?'

'He's fine,' her mother said reassuringly. 'How are you, darling?'

'Fine too, but I've had an unsettling visit from the man who got me out of Sant'Rosa.'

Censoring heavily, she told her mother why Guy had come, ending with, 'I think I'll come home as soon as I can.'

'No,' Isabel said firmly. 'You need that holiday, Lauren—your health isn't anything to take lightly.'

'I feel perfectly normal again,' Lauren assured her. Well, apart from worrying about journalists, the marriage, and obsessing about Guy. 'But if some reporter finds out about this wretched marriage they'll probably come looking for you.'

After a silence in which her mother absorbed the implications, Isabel responded with even more firmness, 'So we will just ignore them.'

Lauren said bleakly, 'They might start digging around.'

The hesitation at the other end of the line revealed that her mother had already thought of that. 'They won't find anything,' Isabel said finally, her voice taut but confident. 'If this false marriage does come to light, it will be a three days' wonder. Ah, darling—your father's just come in.'

Lauren waited tensely, smiling as her father's voice echoed across the world. 'Stay there,' he commanded. 'By the way, what's the man who got you off Sant'Rosa like?'

'Forceful and formidable,' Lauren said lightly. And judgemental.

'Would I like him?'

She laughed. 'Yes, I think you would. You like Marc, don't you?'

'Very much,' he said gruffly. 'Mind you, Marc saved your life, but then, this man might have too. When this bit of a fuss is over, I'd like to shake his hand. Stay there and finish your holiday, Lauren. I want to see colour in your cheeks when you come back.'

'Yes, Daddy,' she said in mock obedience, and heard him guffaw and say goodbye.

He endured his condition like a soldier, gallantly fighting the limitations it put on his life. She said her goodbyes to her mother, and with stinging eyes rang through to the person who handled her travel arrangements. Whatever her parents said, if the marriage ceremony with Guy ended up in the media she wanted to be at home, not stuck on the other side of the world.

Frowning at the skyline of Singapore through the hotel window, Guy swore succinctly under his breath.

The man on the other end of the telephone said drily, 'At school I used to envy you the ability to swear in five languages. Now I can swear in twenty. But I still can't pull the birds like you.'

In a level, cold voice Guy said, 'Bloody tabloids.'

'They have a place in life.'

'Bottom feeders. Any idea when it's due to break?'

He could almost hear his friend shrug. 'Tomorrow,' he said succinctly. 'They've got a tasty little piece—the dramatic circumstances of the marriage and that it might turn out to be legal, as well as the insinuation she might be Corbett's mistress. He's always good for copy, and it's always a coup to get the sights on someone as news-worthy and cunning at avoiding we poor hacks as you are. Naturally they want to make the most of it.'

'Naturally,' Guy said lethally, fighting back the urge to kill someone. 'How did you find this out?'

'I have friends in high places,' his friend the war corespondent said airily, adding with a muffled snort of laughter, 'Or low places.'

'OK, Sean, thanks a lot. I owe you.'

'Don't worry, I owe you more. After all, you once saved my miserable life.'

'Forget it,' Guy said briefly, and hung up.

He stood for a long time frowning into space before reaching for the telephone again. With the time distance it would be eight in the evening in New Zealand.

As he dialled a number he recalled the way the sun had shone through the window of Marc Corbett's house, collecting in Lauren's hair so that it fell like a river of molten obsidian around her face, somehow giving a soft, pearly glow to her milk-white skin.

Skin like satin against his hand…

As Mrs Oliver wasn't in the house, Lauren picked up

the receiver. 'Hello,' she said carefully above the noisy thud of her heart.

'Can anyone overhear what we're saying?'

Guy! 'No.' Marc had made sure the communications system was incapable of being bugged. Cold foreboding knotted her inside. 'What's happened?'

'I have it on good authority that the news of our marriage is about to explode onto the front pages.' He waited while her hand clenched on the receiver, then asked sharply, 'Are you there?'

'Yes.' She said crisply, 'Thank you for telling me. I'll ring my parents straight away and let them know.'

'Do they know about the marriage?'

'Yes.'

'Sensible of you to tell them,' he said calmly. 'When do you go home?'

'I'm leaving tomorrow.'

He asked for the details of her airline and arrival time, then said, 'I suggest you change your booking to get off the flight in Rome.'

'That's being paranoid,' she said brusquely. 'I'll be fine. No one will be expecting me anyway—the airline won't tell anyone when I'm due in, and my parents are the only other people who know. They're certainly not going to confide in any nice, inquisitive journalist.'

'Fair enough,' he said calmly. 'Have a safe flight home.'

And he hung up.

Blinking back stupid, unnecessary tears, Lauren put down the receiver. She felt like an animal in hiding, every sense strained to the point of pain while wolves closed in on her.

CHAPTER SEVEN

BUT even though Lauren had prepared herself mentally and emotionally on the long flight, the pack of photographers and reporters that greeted her at Heathrow both shocked and scared her. Light exploded in her face as they bayed her name and took photographs.

'Look this way, Lauren!' 'Hi, Lauren—can you tell us about this marriage to—?' 'Lauren, Lauren, over here!' until command and shouted comment blended into a din that mercifully blocked out individual yells.

Shaking inwardly, she clamped her lips together, tuning them out while she searched for the quickest route through the milling mass. And then salvation arrived, in the form of two burly men stamped with the indefinable mark of security personnel.

'This way, please, Ms Porter,' the largest and most solid one said in her ear while the other commandeered her luggage trolley as a shield.

Locking every muscle against a cowardly impulse to run, she allowed herself to be escorted away from the hordes and along a corridor. They stopped outside a door and the one in front held it open.

Bewildered, Lauren went through.

And stopped as the door closed behind her and Guy Bagaton rose to his feet, big and vital and ablaze with raw power. Her heart jumping in incredulous joy, she managed to say in a brittle voice, 'Oh—hello. I gather that the news has broken?'

'This morning.' He sounded as fed up as he looked,

but his size and that indefinable air of competence and authority was hugely reassuring.

Shivering, she rubbed her arms; the impersonal room reminded her sharply of that other room a world away when she and this man had exchanged the vows that now bound them in a false relationship.

'I see,' she said unevenly. 'I expected interest, but nothing like that pandemonium. How did they know I was coming in today?'

With cold contempt he said, 'There's always someone who'll spill the beans.' Eyes as bright and burnished as fool's gold narrowed. 'You look tired. Didn't you get any sleep on the flight?'

'Not a lot.' And now her head was pounding, excitement and shock producing a wild mixture of sensations: intense relief, because she trusted him to deal with any situation, and a fierce sensual charge honed by absence. 'The plane was seething with high school students embarking on a year's exchange in Europe. They settled down for an hour here and there.'

'I see. Come on, let's go.' Still frowning, he took her arm and steered her towards a boarding bridge.

Although a debilitating combination of exhaustion and astonishment tempted her to let him take over, she croaked, 'What's happening? Where are we going?'

'Dacia.'

Blinking, she wondered where Dacia was, before remembering a small princedom in the Mediterranean Sea. She balked, trying to stop. 'Why?'

With an expression as grim as his voice, Guy exerted just enough strength to urge her on. 'Your parents are already there.'

What on earth was going on? Her mind spun stupidly

so that all she could say was, 'But my father can't travel by air.'

'He can if he has a nurse with him,' Guy told her, escorting her along the bridge. 'He's fine; I've just been speaking to your mother. I'm sorry you had to run the gauntlet back there.'

Summoning the last remnants of common sense, Lauren dug her heels in. 'Wait. I'm not sure this is a good idea. What's going on? Why Dacia, for heaven's sake?'

'Because it's quiet and peaceful and you wanted to be out of the limelight,' Guy said evenly. 'A few days there will see the media frenzy die—there's nothing so stale as last week's news.'

'But I—'

'Your parents agreed that this would be the best idea.'

'But I don't understand—'

He rasped, 'It's all I can do to protect you from the sort of gossip that could destroy your life.'

'What? In this day and age? You've got a very naïve attitude to modern society if you think that a marriage of convenience is going to do more than mildly titillate readers.'

Flint-hard and formidable, Guy said brusquely, 'You're the one who's completely naïve. To start off with, you might as well kiss your career goodbye.'

The pain in her breast solidified into a rock, so big she couldn't breathe properly. 'Don't be ridiculous—'

'Don't be an idiot,' he ground out, eyes cold as frozen fire. 'Unless you've got enough incriminating evidence to blackmail him, Corbett's not going to keep you once he knows that you and I were lovers. And with journalists combing through Sant'Rosa and Valanu, it won't be long before he does know.'

'It won't matter,' she said dully. It hurt that he should still believe that ancient piece of gossip.

And that was dangerous, because she shouldn't care what he thought of her.

Guy said harshly, 'He doesn't strike me as a man who's happy sharing his women, and I doubt if he'd surrender to blackmail.' Contempt darkened his face and thinned his mouth.

'No,' she said, her voice muted. 'He wouldn't.'

They were facing each other like enemies, eyes duelling, tense with antagonism. He despised her. 'So you'll be notorious; no one will take you seriously. You might get offers for television or some sort of modelling, but your career's gone. Face that now. If you lie low on Dacia for a week or so, the fuss will die down and you can regroup.'

Taking her numb silence for consent, he urged her into the cabin. Later, she was convinced that jet lag had scrambled her brain and sapped her will-power; surely that had been why she'd surrendered so meekly to his authoritative handling!

Once inside, a harried glance revealed that the plane was a private one, and they were the only passengers.

'You'll get an excellent view from this window,' Guy said, standing back to let her sink into a superbly comfortable leather seat.

When he leaned down, sensations rioted through her in a delirious mixture of fire and honey and aching need. She swallowed to ease an unbearably dry throat and closed her eyes against the arrogantly angular jaw and the bold male curves of his beautiful mouth.

But as he clicked her seat-belt into place, she couldn't block out the subtle, spicy scent that was his alone. Memories rushed back, of heat and long tropical nights when the evocative, erotic perfume of frangipani blossoms and the drowsy sound of the sea on the reef provided the perfect setting for passion. And of Guy, taking her to heaven with his lean, skilled hands and experienced understanding of what a woman's body needed to drive it to unbearable ecstasy...

He straightened, his hard-edged face shutting her out as effectively as a mask. 'I'm going up to the cockpit. Try to get some sleep.'

With gritty eyes, Lauren watched him walk away, big body moving with a fluid, controlled confidence that came close to arrogance.

What she and Guy had shared was nothing more— nor less—than transcendental sex. Neither then nor in New Zealand had either of them thought about love.

When the door closed behind him she transferred her gaze to the window, not taking in the minor bustle of getting a plane into the air. Surely he couldn't be the pilot?

But why not? He'd known the man who'd evacuated the resort guests from Sant'Rosa. When he wasn't fighting wars did he fly charter planes?

A movement from behind called her attention to a steward, who smiled and offered her a drink.

'Water, please,' she said thickly.

Once he'd brought it and explained the safety features, the plane taxied out onto the runway. She sank back into the seat and let the cool liquid slide down her parched throat until she'd finished the glass.

At cruising height the steward reappeared, offering food and more drinks.

'Just a pot of tea, thank you,' she told him with real gratitude.

She'd occasionally flown in private jets chartered by Marc to get him and his family quickly and privately between New Zealand, where they spent many of their holidays, and Paris, where they lived.

This one, she thought dreamily, had a personal touch that meant someone had cared about its decoration. Elegantly serene, it invited relaxation. She decided she'd like whoever had decided on the colour scheme and the carpet.

Her roving gaze settled on the bulkhead between the cabin and the kitchen. Frowning, she discerned a crest that seemed familiar—a leopard fiercely clawing the air. Something about the outline nagged at her tired mind. She closed her eyes and set about capturing the elusive memory.

The ring! Her lashes flew up. Guy's ring, the one he'd put on her finger at that mockery of a wedding ceremony. Narrowing her eyes, she stared at the crest, superimposing the remembered lines over the leopard.

It fitted exactly.

Brain working furiously, she recalled a faint note of pride in his voice when he spoke of Dacia. Did this plane belong to a Dacian airline?

'Would you like something to read?' the steward murmured after he'd delivered a tray of tea.

'Yes, thank you.'

He arrived back with a couple of extremely expensive-looking fashion magazines.

Just what she needed—something light and cheerful. With stubborn determination she eyed models in what appeared to be designer shrouds before turning the page to read her horoscope, which announced that she'd met the only man she'd ever love.

Lauren shut the magazine with a snap and stared unseeingly out of the window.

Was Guy Dacian? Part Dacian, anyway; he was built on too impressive a scale to be wholly of Mediterranean stock, but genes inherited from that area would explain his olive skin and beautiful mouth.

And a different first language would be the source of the faint intriguing hint of an accent that intensified when he was making love...

More dangerously bittersweet memories burned through her. Hastily she picked up the magazine again. Nothing on the pages could banish flashbacks of days and nights on Valanu—the rich gleam of sunlight on Guy's wet skin, the quick flash of white teeth when he'd laughed, and the note in his voice when he'd spoken her name...

She dreamed about him every night now.

Swift excitement pulsed through her when the door into the cockpit slid back to let him through. So he was part of the crew.

When he stopped to speak to the steward, Lauren watched him uneasily. He looked different—much less of the beachcomber, much more a sophisticated European. And it wasn't just the removal of that stubble. She'd always been aware of his bred-in-the-bone authority, but in the hothouse situation on Sant'Rosa and Valanu she hadn't noticed this cool, urbane detachment.

Now, filling her hungry eyes with the sight of him, she finally accepted something she'd been trying to repress since their first meeting. Some time during their idyll in Valanu she'd slipped over the invisible dividing line between attraction and love.

The knowledge hit with heady impact, sending a tidal

wave of adrenaline rushing through her. For a precious few seconds she allowed herself to savour the exquisite thrill of loving Guy. Then she forced herself to lock that love in her heart and throw the key away.

Because Guy didn't love her. Everything he'd done had been because he was chivalrous and protective. Twice he'd rescued her from unpleasant situations; he'd lent her money and bought her clothes, and he'd made sure she didn't get pregnant. He'd made love to her with heart-shaking tenderness and raw desire, but all that meant was that for those days he'd wanted her—even though he'd believed her to be Marc's mistress.

But lust chose without discrimination and died swiftly. The father she shared with Marc had wanted her mother too—for a week—although he'd been married.

She couldn't let herself love Guy.

He said something that brought a white grin to the steward's face, then turned. Just in time, Lauren fixed her gaze on the magazine in her lap, every sense strung as tight as piano wire. When he was a couple of paces away she forced herself to glance up enquiringly, because ignoring him would be as much a giveaway as gazing at him with her heart in her eyes.

He sat down beside her with a flash of the reckless grin she remembered from Sant'Rosa. 'You English and your tea!'

'Don't Dacians drink tea?'

His smile disappeared. After a taut second he said, 'Not a lot—we mostly drink coffee.'

'You have excellent English.' It was an inane remark, but it was all her scrambled brain could come up with.

'I spent some years at school in England, and I'm fortunate enough to be a good linguist.'

She nodded, thinking of his mastery of the Sant'Rosan language, then donned her coolest composure and looked up into his face. 'Thank you for getting my parents out of that feeding frenzy. I had no idea a media pack in full cry would be so—' she abandoned *frightening* to substitute '—so intimidating.'

'Your parents are sensible enough to see when retreat is the best decision,' he said with a casual lack of emphasis. 'And you still have holiday time, I believe.'

The aloof enquiry in his tone slammed up more barriers. 'Another couple of weeks.'

'You parents said you'd been ill.'

She shrugged. 'A bout of pneumonia. It wasn't very serious, and it's over now.'

'You're still pale.' His voice was deliberate, but an unsettling note in it made her acutely aware of his closeness.

'I'm always pale, and at the moment I'm jet lagged,' she admitted with a wry smile. 'I'll be fine after a good night's sleep.' And to convince him, she finished brightly, 'I've never been to Dacia, but I believe it's beautiful.'

'Every bit as much as Sant'Rosa or New Zealand,' he said ironically, 'although in an entirely different way.'

She relaxed a little while he told her of its blood-stained history and eventual conquest four hundred years previously by a pirate. 'He sailed into the harbour and imposed a rule that was ruthless and autocratic, but surprisingly enlightened for the time.'

'He sounds familiar,' she murmured dulcetly.

He directed an enigmatic glance her way. Her heartbeat shot into overdrive, a wild counterpoint to the drugging sweetness of desire that washed through her, merciless and compelling.

'Are you calling me ruthless and autocratic?' he drawled, eyes gleaming with tawny fire.

Laughter bubbled through her. 'How intuitive of you to guess! Of course you are—you think nothing of ploughing roughshod over anyone who gets in your way.'

'Admit that I always try to convince with sweet reason before I bring in the heavy artillery,' he returned virtuously, the lazy note in his voice belying his words.

'I'll admit no such thing,' she retorted. 'Within a few hours of meeting you I found myself married to you, and I don't recollect any sweetly reasonably discussion then.'

And a few days later she'd been in his bed, willing prisoner of a reckless, desperate passion that overthrew years of restraint and self-discipline.

Yet she couldn't regret it, although the aftermath seemed likely to cause endless complications and heartache. Hastily she finished, 'And now I've been hijacked to Dacia!'

'Some situations call for action,' he observed, straight-faced.

Lauren went very still. 'Yes,' she said, remembering the all-pervasive smell of fear on Sant'Rosa. 'I don't remember whether I actually thanked you for getting me off Sant'Rosa.' She looked up as far as his chin. 'I am very grateful. I know what could have happened if I'd been stuck there.'

'I'd have taken care of you.'

Startled, she took in a face carved of granite, coldly determined, so implacable that a cold finger of foreboding ran down her spine. She'd known him as a beach-

comber, as a man of action, as a lover, but her first
impression had been of a pirate.

Now she suspected that the pirate persona revealed
his true nature.

God, she thought, what have you got yourself into?
You should have stuck it out in London...

She said sombrely, 'I'd have been a nuisance, and as
you pointed out then, I'd have put you in even more
danger than you were already in.'

'It's over now; don't worry about it.' He stood up
and smiled down at her, although his eyes were unreadable. 'Drink up your tea, then try to catnap. I'll see
you once we land.'

Throat aching and tight with repressed emotion,
Lauren watched him go, remembering moments when
she'd lain on the bed in that house in Valanu and
watched him walk towards the glass doors onto the terrace. Sunlight had gilded every powerful curve and line
of his body, the smooth play of muscles, the lean
strength of legs and arms. Unbearably stirred, she had
closed her eyes against him, but that bronze image was
burned into her retina and her heart.

She dragged her mind back to the present with relief.
Both the china and the silverware had the same crest,
the Dacian leopard, she'd noticed as she had poured tea.

If she'd had any sense she'd have asked Guy about
the owner of the plane. Unfortunately her mind shut
down when he came near.

She drank some tea and ate one of the small, delicious sandwiches, then leaned back in the seat and tried
to sleep. It didn't work. Thoughts of Guy tossed through
her mind, so to give her restless brain something else
to chew on, she reached for the discarded magazine and
began leafing desultorily through its pages.

After several moments she realised she'd been staring at one page. Blinking, she focused. Beefcake, she thought as several handsome male faces gazed back at her with varying degrees of interest.

One of them was Guy.

Unable to believe what she was seeing, she shook her head, then gazed again at the photograph. Yes, it was Guy.

He was a *model?*

Stunned, she began to read the text beneath the photograph.

'And the most gorgeous,' it burbled, 'if you like your royalty moody, magnificent and hard to catch, is Prince Guy of Dacia, billionaire…'

Lauren blinked again, her heart contracting into a cold, hard ball in her chest. Royalty? *Prince* Guy?

…and at thirty-two still unmarried and breaking hearts all over the world. We wonder if he'll follow the footsteps of his cousins, Prince Luka, the ruler of Dacia, and Princess Lucia, Mrs Hunt Radcliffe, who both fell in love with New Zealanders.

Prince Guy of Dacia, Lauren thought woodenly, jettisoning hopes she'd barely recognised.

Oh, she knew that name; prince, hugely successful businessman, lover of beautiful women, and reclusive object of intense media interest. She closed her eyes, but when she opened them he was still frowning out from the page.

She'd heard of him, seen photographs—why hadn't she recognised him when she'd met him in Sant'Rosa?

Because stubble had blurred the aristocratic features, and because—well, because you simply didn't expect to find a European prince on an island in the middle of the Pacific Ocean.

And because she'd been so aware of him that she'd temporarily lost her mind!

Why hadn't he told her? She bit her lip. Presumably he expected her to know that Bagaton was the family name of the Dacian royal family. Well, she hadn't.

A turbulent mix of emotions—a stark, wholly irrational sense of betrayal, fury and dark desolation—razed every thought but one from her brain. She had been a complete and utter fool, wilfully ignoring anything that didn't fit her first impression of him.

No wonder the Press had met her with such avid determination at the airport! This jet, with its luxurious seats and its atmosphere of privilege and power, its crested china and silver, was either his or his cousin's—the reigning prince.

The distance between Lauren Porter and their world of birth and privilege loomed like a cliff face, dangerous and insurmountable.

How long would it be before someone started digging into her background? Her stomach tightened as fear kicked in. If they hadn't already begun. She was already linked to Marc; would someone pursue that link and find out that she and her boss were half-siblings?

If anyone made the connections, she'd be revealed as the bastard daughter of Marc Corbett's father, the cuckoo in her father's nest. She could cope with that, but her parents would be exposed to sly, sniggering insinuations that would hurt them unbearably and strain her father's precarious health.

All to sell a few more newspapers…

Trying to swallow the lump in her throat, Lauren stared down at the photograph of Guy. By the forbidding expression of his angular face he'd been furious at being snapped. Setting her jaw, she forced herself to read the rest of the blurb.

Prince Guy is probably the richest of the playboy princes; he inherited millions from his mother, a Russian heiress and great beauty, and he set up his own software firm after leaving university. It now earns him millions each year. Fiercely protective of his privacy, he's also a humanitarian who is interested in ecology.

Lauren closed the magazine and fought back despair. If she'd known who he was, she'd have taken her chances on Sant'Rosa.

As for making love with him—never!

Somewhere deep inside her, a mocking voice laughed. Oh, yes, you would, it mocked. You wanted him desperately. You still do. And you're angry with him because not telling you means he didn't trust you.

Which was ridiculous, because she hadn't trusted him with the entire truth about herself.

Her ears popped as the plane banked and turned. Lauren stared stonily ahead, trying to convince herself that no one would be able to find out that Marc was her half-brother.

It was extremely unlikely that they'd discover that he had donated his bone marrow to her. And why should they search twenty-nine years in the past to discover that her mother and Marc's father had been on the same cruise through the Caribbean?

No, her parents were safe from media prying—and

even if they weren't, Guy had pulled them out of the vortex and into temporary safety.

When the seat-belt sign flashed on with a melodious chime, she relaxed her hands from their death grip on each other in her lap and began to breathe deeply, and out, in and out, until the wild turbulence of her emotions abated. If it killed her she'd be calm, because she didn't dare be anything else.

CHAPTER EIGHT

AT THE Dacian airport the steward escorted Lauren into a private room, empty except for flowers and some comfortable lounge furniture, then went off to get her luggage. She waited tensely until Guy came into the room.

Her heart clenched. You can do this, she told herself with ice-cold resolve, determined not to wilt under his keen scrutiny. You'll be polite and crisp and very, very restrained. You are infatuated with this man, but it won't last, because you won't let it.

She took another deep breath.

Guy said, 'Your luggage will be here in a few minutes. Did you manage a nap?'

'No,' she said, adding with a smile that hurt the muscles in her cheeks, 'I'm fine, thank you.'

He didn't seem to notice anything different about her attitude, but she didn't fool herself. Like every predator, he was acutely tuned to his surroundings.

Neither spoke as they went down in a lift and walked out of the building into heat that sucked the breath from her lungs. Ahead, a limousine purred softly, like a waiting cat. Apart from that and the sound of a jet in the distance, it was blessedly silent. No hounds of the Press yapped around her, no lights flashed in her eyes. A uniformed man gave a short salute to Guy and held the back door open. Behind the wheel she made out the form of a driver.

Sliding into the seat, she commented in a voice with

no expression at all, 'It's every bit as hot as the tropics, but not at all humid.' And because she could no longer hold the question back, she asked with a cool lack of emphasis, 'What exactly were you doing on Sant'Rosa?'

'I have interests there. And friends.' He glanced down at her, thick lashes veiling the glimmering depths of his eyes. His tone told her nothing as he went on, 'Several years ago I spent a few weeks there as a hostage.'

A *hostage?*

Horrified, she asked unevenly, 'How on earth did that happen?'

'I delivered medical supplies during the civil war, and the government of Sant'Rosa saw a way of using me.' He shrugged, looking straight ahead as the car drew smoothly away. 'They kidnapped me to persuade my cousin to act as intermediary between them and the rebels.'

She stared at him. 'What happened?'

'I escaped the second night,' he said nonchalantly. A swift grin reminded her again of the buccaneer she'd first met, as did the wry note in his voice when he added, 'It wasn't difficult; they were pretty half-hearted gaolers.'

She closed her eyes. 'You escaped, but you stayed on the island? In the middle of a civil war?'

'They were desperate,' he said briefly. 'And I liked them. They knew the Republic was ready to move troops across the border if there was any chance of a truce between the warring sides. In fact, we fought off an incursion while I was there.'

Appalled at the risks he'd taken, she demanded, '*We* fought off?'

His broad shoulders lifted. 'I was involved in a very minor way,' he said casually. 'They were much better bush fighters than I was, but terror makes fast learners.'

'Or dead ones,' she said tightly.

'Life's for living; it's not worth much if you're forever looking over your shoulder.'

The car purred quietly down a road shared with an occasional donkey and many more motor-scooters, all ridden by young men with very white teeth who waved insouciantly at the limousine as it eased past them.

Lauren clamped her lips together to stop herself from raging at Guy for valuing his life so cheaply.

'We're heading inland to a villa up in the hills; I thought your parents would prefer it to the coast because it's cooler there,' he told her.

'Thank you.' She had to fight back a heavy thud of disappointment. For some reason she'd thought they'd be at the same place...

Fool! A sensible woman would want as much distance between them as possible.

But she wasn't sensible about Guy. From the moment she'd seen him, villainously unshaven on Sant'Rosa, she'd battled a ferocious, elemental appetite that had nothing, she reminded herself stringently, to do with love or respect.

He said, 'My cousin, Luka, and his wife would like to meet you, but they're sure that you and your father need to rest today, so it will probably be tomorrow.'

'I'll look forward to that,' she said untruthfully.

He lifted a lean hand to acknowledge a wave from a donkey rider. Olive trees shimmered in the slow breeze, their leaves gleaming silver against a sky as blue as heaven. Small plants and wild flowers grew against the bases of ancient stone walls that bordered the road.

Guy surveyed her, his eyes cool and intent. 'What's the matter?'

Lauren gathered her composure around like cling film, leaned back and showed her teeth.

'Nothing,' she said coolly. 'Well, nothing apart from a dodgy marriage to a man who neglected to tell me he was a prince.'

His brows lifted. Wielding courtesy like a weapon, he said with suave distinctness, 'It didn't seem relevant at the time.'

'Most people would consider it very relevant. I had no idea that you were a member of the Dacian royal family until—' she glanced at her watch '—about half an hour ago, when I saw an article about you in a magazine. When we went through that ceremony on Sant'Rosa I did think Bagaton sounded vaguely familiar, but not enough to ring alarm bells.'

'Alarm bells?' he said softly. 'Why should you be alarmed?'

She lifted her head and met his glinting gaze full on. 'I'm not in the habit of marrying princes, even to get out of a bad situation.'

'I didn't tell you because you didn't ask,' he returned with cutting urbanity. 'You found me useful, so you sensibly used me. Besides, it didn't matter—it's merely an accident of birth. The important thing on Sant'Rosa was to get you to safety.' He flicked her a glance edged with satire. 'You didn't ask who I was when I came to you in Valanu.'

Lauren bit back the rash words threatening to tumble from her tongue but couldn't stop herself from snapping, 'I thought I knew who you were.'

'Perhaps,' he said softly, 'I should ask you the real question.'

'Which is?' Although her voice was crisp with hauteur, she knew the moment she said the words that they should never have been spoken.

'Why did you offer yourself to me in Valanu?'

Humiliation burned in her throat. Without thinking she flashed, 'I felt sorry for you.'

His eyelashes drooped and for a frightening second she flinched at the very real menace she saw in the hooded eyes.

But when he said, 'You have a charming—and very effective—way of feeling sorry for men,' his voice was insultingly indifferent. 'Not that it matters. The title is completely irrelevant—apart from affection for my cousins and the islanders, I have only sentimental ties to Dacia. Prince Luka has a very promising four-year-old son, and the prospect of another arriving before the end of the year, so Dacia is well set up without me, a situation I'm more than happy with.'

'Lucky you,' she said, her voice as wooden as her expression. 'All of the deference and no responsibility.'

He shrugged. 'I assume you're blaming me for the Press frenzy at the airport.'

She said quietly, 'No. You could have told me who you were when you came to New Zealand to warn me the marriage might be valid, but I suppose there was always the chance that I might have charged you a handsome sum for a quick divorce.'

'I can deal with blackmailers,' he said on a ruthless note. 'Perhaps I should have told you, but it seems pretentious to announce that I'm a prince to people who couldn't care less.'

'I suppose it is.'

'As for the media—' His voice hardened even more. 'Yes, if I hadn't been who I am I doubt very much if there'd have been any reporters to meet you in London. I'm sorry you got caught up in it, but I'm not answerable for people who like to season their breakfasts with highly suspect gossip about princes and pop stars and sportsmen.'

'Of course you're not,' she said in a toneless voice, feeling small and petty.

He covered her rigid hands with his warm, strong one. 'But knowing who I am wouldn't have made any difference on Sant'Rosa—you'd have married me if I'd had to hold a pistol to your head.'

Her heart picked up speed, the pulse at her wrist fluttering under his fingers.

Of course he noticed. After a charged second he said on a raw note, 'I promised myself I wouldn't touch you.'

Lauren had to force herself to return, 'Then don't. It's not necessary.'

He lifted his hand, but as the car left the main road and began to climb, he said deliberately, 'I don't seem to be able to forget that for a few days we were lovers. Can you?'

Her bones melted as images from those few days flashed across her mind with full sensory impact. Attacked by a bitter regret, she said doggedly, 'It was a time out of time—a lovely tropical fantasy, but now we're in the real world, and it's over.'

His ironic laughter stunned her. She flashed a sideways glance and shivered at the compelling determination of his expression. 'Liar,' he said calmly.

When Lauren opened her mouth to object he sealed her indignant response with his fingertip. Mutely, her body struggling with an overload of sensation, she stared at his arrogant, handsome face.

With that fascinating hint of an accent underlying each forceful word, he said, 'No matter how hard we try to pretend, when I touch you we both feel that electricity. Don't try to convince me—or yourself—that it doesn't exist. What we need to talk about is how we're going to deal with it.'

He removed his finger from her lips and sat back in the seat, his profile an angular, uncompromising statement against the silver-grey foliage of the olive trees lining the road.

With stubborn precision Lauren said, 'We don't do anything about it.'

Still quivering inside, she dragged her head around to stare blindly out of the window, fuming when Guy made no answer. Instead she heard him speak in Dacian through the intercom to the driver. His voice, easy and relaxed, told her that he wasn't suffering any inner turmoil.

Lauren clawed back the tattered remnants of her control. Her father had once told her that the tone of a man's servants told much about the master; listening to the driver, she decided that his respectful reply was entirely free from servility, and that he liked Guy.

Who said no more about the attraction that smouldered between them. Instead, with infuriating self-possession he turned into a tour guide, explaining the age and the reason for various interesting ruins along the way, and discoursing on his cousin's plans for the island.

The villa in the hills was a tall, square house, redeemed from severity by blush-pink walls and shutters in a muted dark green. Gardens stretched around it, the trees and arbours melding inconspicuously into olive groves.

Delighted by its faded charm, Lauren leaned forward a little as the car swung up the drive.

From beside her Guy observed, 'According to family tradition the house was built for the Venetian mistress of one of the nineteenth-century princes. She had an embarrassment of children, but he spent most of his time here.'

Lauren stiffened. 'Why didn't he marry her?'

'He was already married to a very stern woman who never, so the story goes, smiled.'

'I wouldn't smile either if my husband flaunted a mistress in my face,' Lauren said astringently, reaching for her bag as the car slowed down.

The second the words left her mouth she realised she'd made a mistake. Guy's brow lifted and he surveyed her with a twisted smile. 'Is it the infidelity or the flaunting that you disapprove of?'

'Both,' she said shortly, wishing that she could tell him about her relationship with Marc. She couldn't, of course, because it wasn't her secret.

Her mother came out of the shadows beneath the portico, graceful and composed as always, the grey eyes she'd bestowed on her daughter serene and limpid. Nevertheless her smile was a little too set, her movements too careful to be natural.

Hurrying out of the car, Lauren gave her a quick hug. 'How's Dad?'

Isabel smiled at Guy. 'Fine. He's waiting inside for you.'

As Lauren ran up the steps she heard her mother say, 'Guy, thank you so much for organising this— I don't know what we'd have done without you.'

Her tone revealed that she liked him. So did every other woman, Lauren thought with crisp cynicism as she walked into the coolness of the house and found her father waiting in a big drawing room decorated in a subdued palette of cream and ochre and the same silvery green as the olive leaves.

Nothing lushly tropical about this place!

'Hello,' she said and hugged him tightly. He returned it with vigour. Relieved, she pulled back and regarded him. 'So now we know that you can travel by air without any problems,' she observed severely, 'you've no excuse to stay at home in future.'

He smiled at her. 'It seems I need a nurse to keep an eye on me, but I got here in one piece. How are you, darling?'

'A bit groggy from lack of sleep.' Her rapid description of the exchange students' antics made him laugh.

When she finished Guy said from behind, 'I have an appointment in a few minutes, so I must leave now. I hope you enjoy your stay here.'

Flushing, Lauren remembered her manners. 'I'll come out with you.'

He stood back to let her through the door. Once it had closed behind them he said, 'Walk in the garden with me for a few minutes.'

'Why?'

His brow lifted. 'Because it's cooler than standing out on the gravel in the sun. Dacia is not as hot as Sant'Rosa or Valanu, but the sun will burn your white skin.'

Feeling foolish, she said, 'Oh. Yes, all right.'

The garden, throbbing with cicadas, was certainly cooler. In the shade of a dark, dome-shaped tree, Guy remarked with disconcerting shrewdness, 'Satisfied that your father hasn't taken any harm from flying?'

She blinked back tears and gave him a strained smile.

'He looks great. They both do. Guy—oh, in public, should I call you Your Highness?'

'No,' he said tersely, his voice quick and hard and cold.

'I don't want to break any rules,' she said.

He showed his teeth in a smile that held little humour. 'Between us,' he said sardonically, 'we've broken so many that it doesn't matter. The first time you meet Luka, call him Your Royal Highness. After that it's sir, until he tells you not to bother with formality. The same applies to Alexa, although she has a tendency to giggle when anyone calls her ma'am.'

He sounded fed up. Lauren said, 'Thanks. In fact, thank you for everything. I imagine that between us we've made a huge mess of your schedule, and I'm sorry—'

He interrupted with curt impatience, 'Don't be foolish. Naturally I feel responsible for this situation; I shall do what I can to make it easier for you. Now go inside, have a meal, talk to your parents and go to bed as soon as it gets dark. Do you ride?'

She blinked. 'Yes, I do. Well, Pony Club level.'

'Then I'll call for you after breakfast tomorrow morning with a suitable mount,' he said and flicked her cheek with a casual finger. 'Sleep well.'

'No— Guy—that's not a good idea.'

His black brows lifted. 'What? Sleeping? I think it's an excellent idea.'

The lazy, caressing note in his voice set fires smouldering deep inside her. Gritting her teeth, she said, 'I don't want to fuel more media furore. Shouldn't we keep as far away from each other as possible in case the marriage has to be annulled?'

'Discovering that the marriage might be valid hasn't

turned me into a serial rapist,' he drawled in a voice like chipped ice.

Her eyes widened as she searched his hard face. 'I know that, but—'

He cut her off with a total lack of finesse. Every word sharp-edged, he said, 'My cousin Luka is as close to being an absolute ruler as you can get nowadays without aspiring to dictatorship. He's slowly organising a democratic system of government—against the wishes of most of his subjects so far—but at the moment he can ban anyone he doesn't want on the island, and if anyone does sneak in, he can see that they get shown politely off.' He frowned, but his voice softened as he said, 'Why do you think I brought you here?'

Lauren said doubtfully, 'I hope you're right,' then made the mistake of smiling at him.

Her heart kicked into high gear when he smiled back. Experienced and wicked, that killer smile promised untold delights—delights that figured largely in her dreams each night, so that she woke hot and aching with frustration.

How long would it take for the Press to forget them? If she had to stay here for more than a week she'd be in real trouble...

He bent his head and kissed her cheek, a touch so light there was no reason for her bones to melt.

The heat in his eyes transformed into cynicism. 'As for the Sant'Rosans, don't worry about them. Believe me, they're not in the habit of reading gossip columns. They've got more important concerns to worry about.'

He took her arm and steered her back to the house. At the door he said, 'Get a good night's rest. Shadows under your eyes don't suit you.'

*   *   *

Towards morning Lauren opened her eyes, only slowly realising that she was staring at the tester of a massive four-poster bed. The fabric was arranged like the roof of a tent, fastened in the centre with a medallion carved in high relief.

A leopard.

She was in Dacia, and she was in love with a prince.

No, she was not in love—she was besotted, infatuated, in lust, smitten by the man, but never in love! As soon as she got back to work she'd see it for what it was—a temporary sexual bewitchment, so fierce it would burn out in the routine of ordinary life.

In other words, exactly what her mother had felt for the man she'd taken as a lover for one crazy week. Isabel had always loved Hugh Porter; when she'd come to her senses she'd gone back to him.

Lauren frowned and wondered why it was so hard to convince herself that all she felt for Guy was that temporary flash and dazzle.

Because he'd shown himself to be brave and chivalrous? Or something so simple as being able to make her laugh?

Whatever, she couldn't let it affect her. Fairy stories were for children; she wasn't a Sleeping Beauty and Guy was too tough and autocratic to be a fairy prince, and there'd be no happily-ever-after for them.

The bleak truth hurt, but not facing it would lead to greater pain; better to accept it, ignore the heartache and get on with her life. But oh, it would have been so much easier to deal with if she'd been able to go cold turkey. This stay on Dacia was going to be refined and subtle torture.

Thank heaven the media's voracious appetite for stories soon burned out!

Yet she couldn't regret meeting Guy. As for making love with him—the thought of never knowing that extreme pleasure made her shudder.

A wistful fantasy drifted across her mind; for a few minutes she indulged herself in the tormenting memories, but self-preservation forced the dangerously seductive images from her mind. Instead, she wondered what had happened to her laptop computer in Sant'Rosa; if she had it here she'd be able to contact Marc in the Seychelles. She should warn him that their relationship might become public knowledge. Besides, she'd like the benefit of his ability to cut concisely through to the heart of any matter.

Eventually she drifted off to sleep again, to wake with a thick head and a sombre mood.

In contrast, her father had never looked better across the breakfast table. Any pain, she thought with renewed determination when she ran upstairs to change into the jeans and cotton jersey she'd bought in New Zealand, would be endurable if it kept him safe.

A knock on the door heralded her mother. 'You look much better,' Isabel said with a smile that faded too quickly.

'So does Dad.'

Her mother's voice softened. 'He loves this weather. In fact, he seems to have taken a great liking to Dacia itself. Darling, I'm so glad you're here. I'll never be able to thank the prince enough for rescuing you both times, from Sant'Rosa and then from those journalists.' Her gaze lingered on Lauren's face. 'He was wonderful yesterday—just took over and organised us so smoothly onto the plane and over here. Your father likes him very much, and so do I. What do you think of him?' she finished casually.

Lauren's heart contracted. Infusing her tone with wry briskness, she said, 'I'm very grateful to him, but he's too much like Marc—inclined to take over.'

Another knock on the door produced one of the maids, to tell her with a broad, significant smile that Prince Guy had arrived to take her riding.

'Make sure you put on sunscreen,' her mother said automatically, then laughed. 'I know, I know—modern cosmetics have sunscreen in them. I suppose I'll stop being an over protective mother when you marry. Really marry, I mean.'

The taut note in her voice made Lauren say steadily, 'That's not on the agenda at the moment.'

After a second's hesitation Isabel returned, 'I hope that when you meet a man you can love, you won't let any considerations weigh on you but your chances of a happy life with him.'

Their eyes met. 'When I meet him,' Lauren said quietly, 'I'll let you know.'

Her mother nodded.

Guy was mounted on a chestnut gelding; he rode, Lauren thought for one dazzled moment, like a centaur, at home on the animal in a way she'd never achieve. As she came out into the sunlight a groom dismounted from another gelding with an amiable face and two white socks.

After greeting them both, Lauren swung into the saddle and spent the next few minutes concentrating on staying in the saddle. Guy monitored her carefully, riding close enough to help if things went wrong, and proffering only advice she needed.

She had never felt so safe, she thought despairingly.

At last, confident she could cope, she gazed around. She felt reborn, her worries temporarily allayed by the sheer delight of riding with Guy through a morning all gold and blue and freshly flower-scented, the sea a swathe of purple silk stretching away from the coast.

When the silence grew too intimidating, she could think of nothing more intelligent to say than, 'This horse has a lovely temperament.'

'He's the nursery horse.' Effortlessly Guy controlled his mount, which was trying to take evasive action against the shocking pink flowers of a cyclamen.

Lauren gave a wry grin. 'Entirely suitable.'

'Next time we'll find you something better than old Carlos here—you ride well enough to try something less like a slug.'

Ridiculous that a simple compliment should make her colour like a schoolgirl! She hadn't blushed for years, yet Guy had only to look at her and she went as scarlet as any tomato. 'That's unkind to Carlos—he's a very sweet-tempered slug,' she said, adding, 'I'm nowhere near as expert as you.'

'In our family,' Guy told her drily, 'we're expected to ride before we can walk.'

Indeed. Her pleasure plummeted. His world of high society and the upper echelons of business didn't connect in any meaningful way with hers; although Marc was perfectly at home in that rarefied atmosphere, she'd never socialised publicly with him in case it gave rise to speculation—a precaution that had clearly failed.

Her eyes skimmed Guy's arrogant profile; he was all aristocrat today, and she sensed an aloofness that hadn't been there before. Had the villa, the love nest, been an indication of what he wanted from her? No, she thought grimly, not with her parents in residence!

Yet in spite of the icy splash of down-to-earth practicality, she looked around at a world more sharply experienced, so brightly coloured, the soft ruffle of breeze on her skin so perfumed, the birdcalls so lyrical, that until then she might have been living under a shroud.

'Is all of Dacia as lovely as this?' she asked.

'*I* think so,' Guy said. 'But then, I'm biased. What's your favourite place?'

'A bluebell wood in spring,' she told him promptly, adding without guile, 'But I love Paris in all seasons.'

'Sentimental memories?' he drawled, each word sharp and lethal as a blade of steel.

Was he jealous? No, that was probably too strong a word, but he might be possessive; he'd know Marc lived in Paris.

CHAPTER NINE

LAUREN said coolly, 'My parents took me there for a holiday when I was eight. We arrived at the Arc de Triomphe on Bastille Day, and I lost my heart. Whenever I've gone back I've always found something new and wonderful to love.'

The horse jogged placidly beneath her, ears turning back every so often. Beneath the olive trees the grass was starred with flowers, blue, white, crimson and scarlet, some she recognised and many she'd never seen before.

In a neutral voice Guy said, 'Your—employer—is half-French, I believe.'

'Indeed he is.' The maternal half; their mutual father had been a New Zealander. She straightened her back and said brightly, 'I love riding through a flowery meadow like this, but it seems a shame that the horses crush the flowers.'

'They're resilient. Would you like to canter?'

'If I remember how.'

To her pleasure it came easily. 'It's like riding a bicycle—you truly don't forget,' she said, delighted and glowing when they'd arrived at their destination, a rocky meadow, its grass eaten short by goats, with a magnificent view out over the coast. Distant and dim on the horizon sprawled the indigo shadow that was the mainland of Europe.

After they'd dismounted to tether the horses in the shade of a clump of cypresses, she walked beside Guy across the sweet-scented grass and remarked, 'There's something special about islands— I wonder what it is.'

'Freedom,' Guy stated, turning to point out a couple of smaller islets off the coast of Dacia. 'Islands represent some hidden mystery, places out of time and ordinary life. Almost anything might happen on an island—why do you think Pacific nations spend so much effort repelling would-be beachcombers?'

Lauren's gaze lingered on the powerful male triangle of shoulders sloping down to narrow hips, and the strong curves of his muscled thighs. Sensation pulsed through her like lightning—dangerously beautiful and so powerful she was helpless before it.

Speaking quickly, she said, 'You're probably right. Perhaps it's the beaches that bring out the adventurer in all of us.'

'Are you suggesting that it was the sand and coconut palms on Valanu that persuaded you into my bed?' he drawled, steel underlying the lazy words.

Lauren kept her gaze fixed on the white line of the distant coast while she sat down on a sun-warmed rock. 'You know it wasn't.'

He said brusquely, 'I spoke to my solicitor last night.'

Lauren swallowed. 'And?'

'It's not good news. The marriage is legal, and an annulment is not possible as we've already consummated it.'

A bewildering mixture of regret and chagrin lent an edge to her involuntary response. 'I wish none of this had happened!'

'No more than I do, believe me.' His voice was flat and judicial.

Lauren looked down at her hands. Although he'd

agreed with her, his reply had hurt. 'So what do we do now?'

'We accept it,' he said crisply. He overrode her outraged protest with forceful authority. 'And we announce a date for the formalisation of our marriage in the cathedral here.'

She jumped to her feet and advanced on him, hands clenched at her sides. 'No! I won't accept—'

His regard, cold as frozen sunlight, silenced her. 'Yesterday while we were flying here one of the more noisome English tabloids splashed details of the days we spent together in Valanu across its front page.' His impersonal voice made his next words all the more outrageous. 'The only way to protect you from the gossip and innuendo that's already building is for us to acknowledge the marriage.'

Images of the days and nights spent in his arms jostled through her mind, bringing bright, fleeting colour to her pale skin. She snatched a glance, noting with savage anguish that he'd lost none of his trademark self-assurance.

Pain splintering inside her, she shook her head. 'I can tough this out, and I'm sure you can. After all, this is not the first time you've taken a lover and been outed in the Press.'

'It's the first time my lover had no idea what she was getting into,' he said abrasively. 'If you'd known who I was it wouldn't matter so much.'

So he believed that, even if he believed nothing else. Relief lightened her mood for a second, but his next words darkened it again.

'We'll play it whichever way you choose, but I suggest we stay married for a couple of years. After that you can have a divorce. Of course, I'll make sure that you'd never have to worry about money again.'

'Pay me off, you mean? No, thank you.' Lauren had to articulate each word carefully, gauging her tone to hide how much his pragmatic suggestion hurt. 'Marrying you is out of the question.'

His expression hardened. 'Lauren, we are already married. Nothing is going to change that but a divorce, either now or in two years' time. Before you say any more, you'd better have a look at a sample of the sort of garbage that's being printed.'

He pulled a folded newspaper from his back pocket and handed it over to her.

'Is This Marriage For Real?' it demanded, beside photographs, the one of her a startled mask snapped at the airport.

Appalled, Lauren scanned the page.

'Exclusive details. Tropical Love Nest for Prince and His Commoner Bride.'

Nausea gripping her, she closed her eyes, but cold courage forced her to open them again and read on. Someone had interviewed the charming family who owned the beach shack, and from their replies had cobbled together a tissue of vulgar innuendoes and speculation.

Once she trusted her voice enough to speak, she said distastefully, 'I suppose it could have been worse.'

'Not much.' Anger ran like a rapier blade through the two words.

She shrugged and handed the newspaper back to him. 'It makes no difference,' she said in her most distant tone.

'To what?'

'To my answer to your pro—proposition.'

'It was a proposal,' he snarled.

'For all the wrong reasons.'

Of course he picked her up on that. 'So are there right reasons?'

Although it hurt so much she had to dredge every word from deep inside her, she said tensely, 'I don't want a marriage that means nothing and is programmed to destruct in a couple of years.'

'You weren't so fussy on Sant'Rosa,' he pointed out brutally.

She lifted her hands as though to ward off a blow, then let them drop. 'I know,' she admitted. 'I am truly grateful—'

'I don't want your gratitude!' Guy said between his teeth.

Stiffly she continued, 'I didn't foresee such repercussions. I just want this to be over so I can go back to my real life.'

A line of colour darkened the exotic sweep of his cheekbones. 'And forget that I ever met you? Can you do that?' he asked silkily.

He didn't touch her—didn't even make a movement towards her—but she felt the compelling force of his will-power lock around her like fetters. The temptation to give in was so strong she almost took a step towards him.

That was when she accepted that if she stayed in this marriage she'd fall irrevocably in love with a man who didn't love her. This fierce passion would drive them into each other's arms, and at the end of the two years she would walk away with a shredded heart into a future without hope.

She didn't dare risk such a death of the spirit. 'I can try,' she said tautly. She gripped her shaking hands behind her back and stared at him, eyes darkly desperate. 'Guy, I *can't* do this. I don't know how to behave in your world.'

His brows drew together. 'Alexa is extremely popular, yet she was not brought up to be a princess. She learned; so will you.'

To the sound of her heart splintering, Lauren said childishly, 'You can't force me to.'

He grinned, darkly dominating, dangerous and fiercely attractive. 'I think I could,' he said slowly, 'but it won't be necessary.'

Taking the biggest gamble in her life, she said abruptly, 'I am not who you think I am. Marc Corbett is my half-brother as well as my employer. My mother had a week-long affair with his father, and I'm the result.'

With shoulders held so rigidly they hurt, she scanned his impassive face while seconds ticked by, broken only by a whicker from one of the horses, and the cry of some bird, haunting and lyrically tragic in the warm air.

By the time Guy spoke her nerves were wound so tautly she jumped at the sound of his inflexible words. 'I see. However, it makes no difference. It's common knowledge that Luka's wife, Alexa, is the result of an affair between the then Crown Prince of Illyria and her grandmother.'

'I'm sure it helps if the product of a liaison can claim royal blood,' she said quietly. 'I can't.'

His next words astounded her. 'Does your father—Porter—know?'

She bit her lip, but she'd started this. 'He found out after I had leukaemia.'

At his silence Lauren glanced up. The boldly chiselled angles and planes of his face revealed neither condemnation nor interest—nothing but a concentration that sent a swift scurry of foreboding down her spine.

'So she kept quiet and let your father think you were his child.' Although Guy's tone was neutral, she picked up the note of contempt.

'I'm not going to judge my mother—' she retorted, her voice forbidding him to go any further.

Guy cut her off. 'It is a terrible thing—to deceive a man into believing that the child he loves and cherishes and protects is blood of his blood, bone of his bone, breath of his body.'

She looked at him pleadingly, and then sighed. 'Yes, but in every way that counts, I am his daughter. He convinced me of that after I'd recovered.'

'That is obvious. Thank you for telling me, but it makes no difference.' He smiled without humour and came over to her, taking her cold hands in his.

Her fingers trembled. 'But if anyone finds out—'

His broad shoulders moved in a shrug. 'I will protect your parents as much as I am able,' he said indifferently, and lifted her hands to his mouth, kissing the palm of one, the wrist of the other, smiling with cool satisfaction when she flinched at the sudden thunder in her blood.

Wounded by the calculation in the kisses, she protested, 'Don't you dare try to use sex to influence me.'

'Could I?' he asked in a low, dangerous tone that lifted the hairs on the back of her neck.

'No,' she said untruthfully. Her body was ready for him now; if he wanted, she'd lie down in the flowery meadow and let him take her.

'Liar,' he said, but he let her go. In a level, uncompromising voice he said, 'Luka spoke to me this morning. Last night he was visited by a deputation of islanders. They think the whole affair hugely romantic, but they were adamant that they want our marriage formalised here on Dacia.'

Lauren walked across to where the horses were tethered in the shade. When the gelding lifted his head she stroked the soft nose, desperately fighting a darkness that threatened to overwhelm her. 'I thought your cousin could keep the media under control.'

'He has no power over the airwaves, and the television sets on the island can be tuned into Italian stations, which are full of the news.' He paused, then said deliberately, the faint intonation of his native language in his accent suddenly stronger, 'I would lose respect—and so would Luka—if the people here believed that I used the excuse of a marriage ceremony to take a lover and then dump her. It would be seen as a deliberate flouting of the sacredness of marriage vows.'

Lauren swallowed to ease a mouth suddenly gone dry. 'I can understand the personal aspect of this, but why would your cousin lose any respect?'

'Because he is my cousin, and he is the head of the family. On Dacia, that matters; he would be seen as not wielding proper authority over me, and if a man cannot control his own family, why should his people trust him to rule them fairly?'

'But that's mediaeval!' she protested.

Guy said austerely, 'They haven't had the benefit of democracy. Luka hopes very much that he or his son will eventually be able to relinquish the sole responsibility for the future of Dacia, but of course he wishes to make sure a democratic system is in place first. For that he needs time and the confidence of the people.'

Lauren closed her eyes. She thought raggedly, I can't fight this.

For Guy to lose his reputation like this would scar the part of him that had been brought up to feel an inherited duty towards the islanders.

All she had to weigh against that duty was her heart, and that was far too light to balance the scales. She couldn't allow the personal misery of unrequited love to stand against his hopes for the future of the islanders, made more poignant because they both had firsthand experience of the terror that could inflict people unprepared for independence.

But because she was a fighter, she drew in a ragged breath and made one last effort. 'So he's leaning on you to ratify a marriage of state convenience?'

Guy's broad shoulders lifted in a shrug. 'I am not easily leant on, and Luka would not do so, but I understand the situation and I agree with him.'

The iron jaws of a trap edged closer. 'This is important for you, isn't it.' It wasn't a question.

He was silent so long she turned her head to look at him. With painful honesty, Lauren thought he had never looked so forbidding—a man accustomed to wielding authority and power faced with a distasteful decision.

A man who'd accept a fake marriage out of a sense of duty. Would he take a mistress, as his distant ancestor had done?

No, she thought, her heart a stone in her chest. His honour wouldn't allow that.

Sunlight conjured fire from his dark hair as he gave a short nod. 'I owe my family and the people of Dacia my best efforts.'

It hurt so much her breath locked in her throat, but she managed a humourless smile. 'So I was wrong when I said you got the deference without the responsibility. Why is this so important to the Dacians?'

'They are a conservative, religious people; they hold marriage vows in high esteem.'

He didn't say that none of this would be happening if she hadn't seduced him on Valanu. He didn't have to, just as he didn't have to say that her parents would hate the speculation her continued refusal would have caused.

Defeat bitter in her mouth, Lauren swung around and walked away to look out over the rocky hillside to the settled lands below, rows of olive trees and grapevines making patterns across the countryside.

Like her mother, she had followed her heart to danger. If she'd kept her head she wouldn't be in this situation, heading knowingly into a love that could only hurt and humiliate her.

Because it was important to him, she would agree. She said in a muted voice, 'Then it seems that I have no choice. It isn't fair that you should pay for something I did.'

'What?'

She lifted her chin. 'Seducing you on Valanu.'

The sudden glitter in his eyes surprised her, but not as much as his uncompromising inflection when he said, 'You gave me passion and warmth and tenderness; you showed me that there is more to the world than the casual brutality I'd seen on Sant'Rosa. Although I knew it intellectually, I found that knowledge in your arms.'

Lauren said quietly, 'And I didn't make love to you because I felt sorry for you.'

His smile was ambiguous. 'It doesn't matter. I could have walked away from you, so we are in this together, Lauren. This marriage is not something you made happen because you got carried away by the tropical moonlight and the scent of frangipani.' He turned and said abruptly, 'Luka's Press secretary can announce the date tomorrow.'

She said bleakly, 'And afterwards? What then?'

'That,' he said calmly, 'is entirely up to you. If you desire to live here, I own a house on the coast that will be yours for as long as you wish, but I also have houses in London and New York.'

And one in Valanu, she thought. But he still hadn't answered the real question. *What sort of marriage will it be?*

In his eyes glinting gold and amber and tawny shades mingled into heat and fire. 'If the story of your birth is uncovered marriage with me will give you the position to fight anyone who dares slander your parents. I have power, and I will use it on your behalf.'

Lauren tried to form the words she should say, but her tongue wouldn't utter them and her throat wouldn't let them past the lump lodged halfway down it. She knew she was going to agree, because she loved him and this was important to him.

Eventually she said quietly, 'All right.'

Guy gave a low laugh and kissed her, and she kissed him back, even as her heart wept.

When he released her she shivered, but held her head high.

'Don't look so tragic, Lauren.' He sounded sardonic. 'I suggest we go back to the villa now. We'll leave other decisions to a time when both of us are more relaxed.'

He was a fantastic lover and a man with more charisma in his little finger than most other men had in their whole bodies. Her parents liked him very much. Lauren knew he was brilliant, and a hard but fair businessman, but she hadn't known he was a prince until yesterday.

Presumably he had other secrets. And she had just agreed to marry him.

Back at the villa he refused her mother's offer of lunch, but asked if his cousin's wife, Princess Alexa, might call on a short, private visit the next afternoon.

'How very kind of her,' Isabel Porter said. 'We'd love to meet her and thank her for offering us sanctuary.'

'She'll probably want to photograph you,' he warned, amusement glimmering in the topaz depths of his eyes. 'She's brilliant.'

'I saw her exhibition in London—absolutely superb.' Isabel was excited.

Guy nodded, smiling at her with such blatant, unbarred charm that Lauren didn't blame her mother for blinking and going under.

He said, 'You'll like her—she's entertaining and intelligent with the kindest heart in the world. She wishes very much to meet you.'

He looked past her mother to Lauren, still and quiet and very composed. Sunlight pouring through the windows lent warmth to her white skin. She smiled at him, yet he sensed tension beneath her confident exterior, something defiant about the way she met his eyes.

Because they both knew that his touch brought swift colour to her skin, and that when he kissed her that delectable mouth softened and gave him everything he wanted.

And he'd better get the hell out of here, because he wanted her now, warm and willing and eager, lost in ecstasy in his arms.

But first, he had to make the decision he'd forced from her irrevocably.

He said bluntly, 'Mr and Mrs Porter, Lauren and I

have something to tell you. We plan another ceremony in the cathedral to regularise the marriage that took place on Sant'Rosa. I hope you will give us your blessing.'

Hugh Porter said, 'It seems the most sensible decision.' He gave Guy a look that made Lauren's spine snap straight, and finished grimly, 'It saves me from borrowing a shotgun.'

As Lauren choked on the coffee her mother exclaimed, 'Hugh!'

Guy said coolly, 'I don't blame you, sir. I shall look after Lauren to the best of my ability.'

Lauren glared at her unrepentant father, heart twisting at the effort with which he was holding himself together.

Guy stood up. 'Alexa's visit will be the first of a round of social engagements for you,' he said. He didn't look at Hugh Porter as he went on, 'It will be a busy month, but not too exhausting, I hope.'

'I can manage,' Hugh said abruptly.

After a keen glance, Guy nodded. Formally, he said, 'I have to fly to America this afternoon, so I will see you again in about three days. Until I get back, enjoy Dacia in the spring.'

CHAPTER TEN

THE visit from the princess went off well; warm and lively, she talked photography with Isabel, Italian literature with Lauren's father, and exchanged reminiscences of New Zealand with Lauren.

But Lauren knew that behind the charming façade the princess was summing her up, and when she suggested casually that they might like to come to the Little Palace for lunch in a couple of days' time, Lauren wished there were some way of refusing.

Of course they had to go, so it was arranged.

That night, when they were alone together, her mother said in a tone she tried hard to make casual, 'Lauren, are you sure you want to marry Guy?'

'Utterly sure!' Lauren told her, glad it was the truth. She met her mother's scrutiny and added with a wry smile, 'With all my heart. Just not this way.'

Concern glimmering in her eyes, Isabel said quietly, 'I guessed as much. How does Guy feel?'

'That it's his duty to do this.' In a steady voice she sketched in the conversation she and Guy had had.

'And that hurts?'

Lauren bit her lip. 'Yes.'

'Swift passions often die as quickly as they flare up.'

Lauren knew her mother was remembering the long-ago affair that had led to her own conception. 'At first I thought that's all it was,' she said steadily. 'But I— well, it's not just the sex.'

'Oh, darling.' Isabel got to her feet and came over,

giving her a swift hug. 'You must not feel you have to marry him just because you have been lovers. Gossip is unpleasant, but it invariably fades. And no one ever died of embarrassment.'

'I know the difference between sex and love,' Lauren said simply. She drew in a deep breath and at last admitted it to herself as well as to her mother. 'I do love him. I feel for him what Paige feels for Marc—what you feel for Dad.' A smile trembled on her lips because it was the first time she'd said it out loud. 'It's real, I promise. Beneath that formidable exterior he's kind and brave and honourable.'

Isabel frowned, saying drily, 'I know about the brave and honourable parts of his character. They're wonderful qualities, but a husband needs a little more than that.'

'I think we can take his intelligence for granted,' Lauren said, brows knitting as she tried to find the right words, 'and he can laugh at himself. He makes my bones melt and my blood sizzle. I want to spend the rest of my life with him.'

But it wasn't going to happen. Not many people, she thought, had married with the date of the divorce already set.

For Guy it was a winning situation. He'd keep his honour in the eyes of his countrymen, he'd have great sex on tap, and in a couple of years he could wash his hands of her and find himself someone with the right bloodlines to be a suitable bride.

Her mother got to her feet and smoothed down her skirt. 'In that case, there's nothing to be said. Whatever you do, your father and I will back you.' She paused until Lauren nodded. 'Have you let Marc know?'

'Yes,' Lauren said, summoning a smile. 'He was like

you, not at all convinced I know what I'm doing, but Paige and I managed to talk him out of flying here to see what was going on. He settled for coming to Dacia as soon as they get back from the Seychelles.'

That night, in her lovely, subtly decadent room, Lauren tried to relax the tension that gripped her. A bath didn't work, and neither did a surprisingly pleasant herbal tea one of the maids offered.

'For a sore heart,' she said, with a smile that indicated she knew why Lauren had been restlessly pacing around the garden in the darkness. 'It will help you sleep.'

But after drinking it to its dregs, Lauren still felt wired, every cell in her body filled with frustrated longing. In the end she stood at the window and stared out across the gardens and the olive-furred hills.

Owls called in the perfumed dusk beneath stars that burned with a hard white fire. A mile or so away stood the Little Palace, so named because Dacia's other palace, now part museum, part administrative and ceremonial centre, was a huge mediaeval pile built on an ancient Roman fortress that protected the harbour.

It was from the Old Palace that the bald Press statement of the marriage had been issued the previous day. Newspapers had garnished the announcement with speculation, but she and her parents had been protected from any direct contact.

Her painful craving for Guy, so dark and urgent it ached in the core of her heart, produced an instantly muffled sob.

When exhaustion at last closed her eyes in brief, unsatisfying slumber, she fell prey to erotic dreams, all of them starring Guy as he'd been on Valanu, and woke the next morning with heavy eyes that mimicked the state of her spirits.

Action would clear her head and lighten her spirits. And she knew where to go. A few minutes later she slipped through the silent house, her bathing suit covered by one of her sarongs. Early though it was, the first cicadas of the day were already tuning their small zithers.

Halfway down the garden a swimming pool was sheltered behind thick conifer hedges. Elegant and formal with a fountain trickling into one side, it had been built many years before, perhaps for that long-ago prince who'd disported in the villa with his mistress and their large brood.

Ironic, really—the mistress had probably yearned for the security of marriage, whereas Lauren would gladly swap marriage for Guy's love.

The water was still cool, but she dived in and swam methodically, counting out the laps until self-preservation forced her out.

Well, action hadn't worked; drying herself in the tiled bathing cubicle, she accepted that only going cold turkey on Guy Bagaton would exorcise him from her mind and her heart.

'And because of a nation of people you don't know, whose language and culture you don't understand, you can't do that. You're trapped!' she told herself, fastening the sarong above her breasts.

But this ceremony with Guy wasn't for the Dacians; she'd do it because she loved him, and because it was important to him, part of the commitment to honour and duty she admired in his character.

She picked up her hat and towel and walked out into the sunlight, the cold emptiness of her heart a painful contrast to the sensuous heat that caressed her bare shoulders. Emerging into the wider sweep of the garden, she stopped to admire the acrobatics of a pair of tiny birds with gold crests foraging upside down in the dense branches.

Smiling, she watched for a few seconds before a creeping sense of being overlooked tightened her skin; she straightened and turned, and there was Guy striding along beneath the trees, his big, powerful body striped by the sun in tiger shades of amber and black.

Joy burst into life inside her, incandescent and overpowering; she had to bite the corners of her mouth to stop herself from smiling with sheer delight.

He didn't kiss her; instead he examined her with a deliberation that sent little shivers of sensation scudding the length of her spine. 'You don't seem to be making a good job of shifting those shadows under your eyes,' he finally said.

'Whereas you look fine.'

The brilliant tawny eyes softened. 'Do you want to call it off?'

For a moment she didn't believe she'd heard what he said. She stared blankly at him, and his beautiful mouth twisted into a mirthless smile.

'If this business is going to drive you into a decline we'll finish it now.'

Lauren fought with herself before saying tonelessly, 'And what about the Dacian sensibilities you waxed so eloquent about only a few days ago?'

Although he shrugged broad shoulders, his eyes were hard. 'They'll be hurt.'

She said something in French, and he laughed softly and caught her and kissed the word from her lips, and said against them in the same language, 'You have a superb accent.'

'So do you,' she muttered. Words jostled in her head,

but none made the trip from brain to tongue; sickened and humiliated, she closed her eyes.

And then warmth enveloped her, and his strength supported her.

'Please—no,' she whispered, but it was too late. He kissed her forehead and then a vulnerable temple, and she—oh, she surrendered shamefully, without protest, to the unexpected tenderness of his embrace, her heart surging into overdrive in response to the thunder of his.

He said harshly, 'I don't blame you for never wanting to see me again—because of me you've had your life turned upside down.' He cupped her chin and tilted it so that he could look down into her face. 'But I'm no sadist. I hate to see the shadows under your eyes.'

'I don't go back on my promises.' Lauren swallowed. 'And if we cancel now, there'll be an orgy of speculation. My father won't care for himself if the truth about my parentage is discovered, but he'll hate for my mother to face the humiliation. I'm not prepared to put him through that stress.'

Guy released her. 'If you've made up your mind,' he said crisply, 'stop drooping, or people are going to wonder if I beat you.'

She said between her teeth, 'Has anyone told you that you're an arrogant swine?'

He gave a lazy, cynical grin. 'Join the club.'

Of course her mother asked him to breakfast, and of course he agreed. By pasting a thin skin over her emotions and drinking twice as much coffee as usual, Lauren managed to get through the meal, until Guy said, 'I'd like to take you to meet my cousin.'

It was not a request.

Lauren bristled as he went on. 'He is the Prince of

Dacia and the titular head of the family, so it will be
tactful to visit him now.'

Her father forestalled Lauren's acid rejoinder. 'Excellent idea.' He added austerely, 'As your relationship
has been so unconventional, a little propriety won't do
any harm.'

Balked, Lauren wrinkled her nose at him. 'You sound
like a Victorian great-aunt,' she teased.

'At the moment,' he said, but with a dry smile, 'I feel
very much like a Victorian father.'

So it was arranged, but on the way to the Little Palace
Lauren said evenly, 'From now on I'd like you to discuss things with me, not present me with a *fait accompli*
in front of my parents, who, as you well know, think
you're wonderful.'

'Not your father,' Guy said with a sardonic glance.

'You've redeemed yourself.' She didn't trust her
voice enough to say any more.

Thinking about her future filled her with a tearing
mixture of anguish and elation; she swung wildly from
bleak despair to hoping that sharing Guy's bed would
lead to physical satiation and eventual indifference.

Guy turned the car into a gateway, nodding to the
guards, who presented arms and saluted. Lauren froze,
realising for the first time how utterly alien his life was
from hers.

She blurted, 'Will I be a princess?' And could have
bitten out her tongue at the childish naïvety of the question.

'I'm afraid you will,' he said calmly. 'Do you like
emeralds?'

The abrupt change of subject startled her. 'Of course
I like emeralds. They're beautiful.'

'It's a family tradition that each Bagaton bride

chooses an emerald from the treasure house for her engagement ring, but if you prefer another stone, we'll do that.' When she didn't answer he said, 'Crimson suits you superbly, so if you prefer a ruby then that is what you will have.'

'I don't want—'

'An engagement ring is traditional.' A steely note in his voice warned her there would be no compromise. 'Think of it as a costume in a play—it helps to set the mood.'

'An emerald will be fine.' Angry pain drove her to finish, 'I will, of course, return it when the marriage is over.'

His face hardened, but before he could answer she hurried into speech again. 'I'm sorry, that was rude, even though it's true. I'm jittery. What if your cousin hates me?'

Guy sent her a sideways look. 'He'll like you,' he said calmly, and dropped one lean hand over hers, holding them for a second before putting his back on the wheel.

'I'm wondering what I'll do after the—once things settle down,' she said. 'I'm used to working.'

'There is plenty you can do. Charities are always looking for a titled patroness.'

She said restlessly, 'I don't want to just lend my name to things. I need to do something or I'll go mad.'

'Lauren, relax.'

Stiffening her jaw, she looked down at her hands, imagining one of the fabled Bagaton emeralds on her ring finger. If he put it there with love she would wear it with such happiness…

But it wasn't going to happen. Abruptly she asked,

'Do we tell your cousin the real reason for this marriage?'

His jaw tightened into a formidable line. 'No,' he said uncompromisingly. 'Luka and I are great friends, but our relationship, as opposed to our marriage, is none of his business.' He braked, steering the car to the side of the road. 'To anyone who asks, we met on Sant'Rosa, fell instantly in love, and sealed that love during the days we spent together on Valanu.'

Colour drained from her skin, then came flooding back. 'It sounds very romantic,' she said, trying to conceal the misery in her tone with a note of cynicism.

He leaned over and pushed her door open. 'Get out,' he said, straightening up.

Eyes enormous, she stared at him. 'What?'

'Get out,' he said pleasantly. 'You're wound up tighter than a screw. We'll walk a bit so you can use up some of that excess energy.'

It seemed a good idea, so she unfolded herself and pretended to look around at the flowers pushing joyously through the grass.

'And just to make sure we present a convincing face to Luka,' Guy said conversationally, coming up behind her, 'we should do this.'

Hands on her shoulders turned her around; Lauren's gaze flew to a face she didn't recognise, hard with purpose, an implacable will bent on subduing.

'I don't—' she started to say, but the last word was crushed to nothing on her lips and she was lost in a fierce passion that had been starved for too long.

How long they kissed she didn't know, but when he lifted his head she felt bereft and angry and afire with sharp frustration—a turbulent combination of emotions, each fighting for mastery.

And beneath them, the honeyed urgency of sexual anticipation, of need.

Of love.

'Yes,' Guy said, his accent deepening as he scanned her face, 'that looks better.'

She closed her eyes. 'I hate lying!'

His laughter was close to a taunt, but there was a sombre note in his voice. 'You want me—that's no lie. Lack of control is always frightening. I wonder what it is, this strange mixture of need and desire.'

'I read somewhere that it's a cocktail of chemicals in our brains.' If that was so, why did her heart hurt, not her brain?

'I felt it the first moment I saw you.' His hooded eyes were slivers of polished gold, unreadable, compelling.

Shivers of excitement raced down her spine and exploded in the pit of her stomach, but Lauren wasn't ready to admit anything. 'I thought you were a beachcomber.'

Dark brows shooting up, he glanced at his watch. 'We'd better get going.'

But in the car, as she was checking her appearance in her tiny mirror, he remarked, 'A beachcomber?'

Horrified by the feverish glitter in her eyes and the full ripeness his kisses had given her lips, Lauren stroked on lipstick and closed the tube with a fierce turn of her wrist. 'You were arrogant, abrupt and dismissive,' she said with relish.

'So were you.'

She swivelled to stare at his angular profile. The crease in his cheek indicated that he was hiding a smile, but she said indignantly, 'I was just determined to get to that village.'

'You took one look at me and your eyes went dark, and I knew I could have you.'

The lazy satisfaction in his tone catapulted her back to that steamy little resort with the threat of death hanging over it, and the man who'd crossed swords with her there.

'As I said, arrogant,' she retorted. 'And conceited. I wondered if you were there to entertain any single women.'

'A gigolo? What changed your mind?' When she refused to answer, he laughed softly. 'As for who was the most arrogant—that is a question we can discuss at greater length later. For the time being we should leave it, because here is the Little Palace.'

Of course it was huge, a splendid champagne-coloured building, both dignified and appropriate for the Mediterranean landscape.

Swallowing a hard lump in her throat, Lauren eyed the flight of steps that led up to a pillared portico like something out of Rome, and said thinly, 'I don't know what to say to your cousin.'

His swift glance took in her set face. 'You enjoyed talking to Alexa, didn't you?'

She swallowed again. 'Yes, of course—very much.'

'Then you'll like Luka. And it will be mutual. After all, he married a woman with spirit and flair and strength, and fell in love with her when he thought she was what he hated most—paparazzi. Theirs is a true love match.'

Was he wishing this was? His words gave nothing away, and neither did his hard, handsome face. Stubborn pride kept Lauren's spine erect and her shoulders straight as they were shown into the private apartments of the royal family. Only when a delicious small boy came running through the door did she manage to relax a little.

The princess and her son, the grand duke, made any attempt at formality impossible, but Guy's pleasant, inordinately good-looking cousin observed her with a cool interest that missed nothing. He was, Lauren thought unhappily, reserving judgement.

It seemed he might have made up his mind when, just before they left, he said, 'If your parents approve, we will have the formal ceremony at the cathedral, not in the palace chapel, so there will be a parade of carriages through the streets. Dacians love to celebrate, and after this there will be no more royal weddings until the next generation grow up.'

Lauren's expression must have revealed more than she wanted, because Alexa laughed.

'A formal occasion in Dacia isn't like formal occasions anywhere else, Lauren—you'll be fine. I can help you make the arrangements.' She patted her still slender waist and added, 'It will give me something to do while this baby grows.'

Lauren produced a smile that hurt her cheeks. 'I have to admit that a private ceremony is more my style, but if you think it's a good idea, we'll do it.'

On the way back to the villa Guy observed, 'That wasn't so bad, was it?'

'No,' she said on a silent sigh. 'Thank you.'

He lifted an ironic eyebrow. 'For what?'

'Your support.' She had felt it all the time, a solid, reassuring stability that could become addictive.

'You didn't need any support,' he said with an assurance she had to envy. 'You did very well—and in case you're wondering, yes, Luka likes you.'

What Lauren had noticed during that royal inspection

was the power of the love between the prince and his wife. They didn't show it in obvious ways, but it was like a chain of gold linking them, subtle, pervasive and unbreakable.

That was what she wanted. And while she was about it, she might as well reach for the moon too. She gazed out of the window at the glowing countryside slipping by.

When, back at the villa, Guy told her parents of Luka's plans for the wedding, Isabel's elegant brows drew together.

'Hugh, how do you feel about this?'

He answered firmly, 'I have no intention of dying, I can assure you, until I have held my grandchildren in my arms.'

Lauren turned her head and stared out of the window to hide eyes that stung. She would never carry a child of Guy's under her heart.

Very smoothly, apparently not at all concerned by the unsubtle reference to children, Guy said, 'In that case, unless there is a reason for you to return to England, we would be delighted if you stayed here until then.'

Isabel said thoughtfully, 'What about clothes for the wedding?'

'The local couturier is excellent,' Guy told her. 'She is Paris-trained. Alexa buys her clothes from her, and it helps the local economy. Tourists flock to buy clothes from the woman who dresses the princess.'

'Oh, yes, of course.' Isabel looked suddenly startled as though she'd just realised that her daughter's life was going to change irrevocably.

'And Alexa asked me to tell you that she is more than happy to help with anything. My cousin Lucia, Mrs Hunt Radcliffe, was a great source of support to her when she came to Dacia to marry, so Alexa is delighted to be able to do this for another princess of Dacia.'

Guy's urbane charm set Lauren's teeth on edge. He was completely convincing in his role as lover and fiancé. He acted, she thought wretchedly as he let his gaze linger on her face, like a man who was truly in love with her.

He left soon after that, but not before making an appointment to collect Lauren in an hour. 'We need a ring,' he said at her startled glance. 'I've organised the jeweller to assemble a few stones that you might like, but as they're in the Old Palace vaults we'll have to go there.'

They were now outside the door. 'I see,' she said numbly.

He gave her a swift, ironic smile. 'Cheer up, my heart—it won't be as bad as it seems at the moment.'

'Is that a promise?'

'Enough, Lauren.' He looked very uncompromising and remote. 'I am sorry if the idea horrifies you, but it is going to happen. Now, try to think about the design of the ring you wish to wear.'

Unable to put her unhappiness into words, she gestured vaguely. 'I don't have any ideas, I'm afraid.'

'I know this isn't what you expected, or wanted. It is not for me, either,' he said with relentless honesty, 'but as we are the two who caused the whole situation, it is only fair that we be the ones who suffer for it.'

She wouldn't let him see how much his words cut. Pasting a smile onto stiff lips, she said brightly, 'You are absolutely right. Guy, I've been thinking. I can use the time we're married to do a master's degree, something I've been planning to do anyway.'

He nodded and slowed down to negotiate an intersection with the main road. 'An excellent idea. We will have to entertain,' he said calmly, 'but there should be plenty of time to work as well.'

The road took them into the heart of the island's port and main city, a bustling little town that had struck a clever balance between catering for tourists and the needs of its own people.

'The treasure house is in the Old Palace,' Guy told her.

Once there, he escorted her to a small room inside the thick walls of the ancient fortress. Someone had arrayed a collection of emeralds on white velvet—glorious stones that condensed every existing green into a glowing intensity. Guy introduced the jeweller, a stocky middle-aged man with patent-leather hair, who glanced professionally at Lauren's hands.

'Beautiful,' he said approvingly. 'I suggest perhaps a classic setting, without too much ornamentation?'

'I'd like that.' Lauren sketched a quick look across the intense fire of the stones, her gaze stopping on one.

Guy picked it up and held it against her hand. 'That one?'

The stone felt cold against her skin, a violent contrast to the warmth of his fingers. Her heart contracted into a knot. 'Yes, that one.'

The jeweller beamed. 'An excellent choice. A glorious stone almost free of flaws. You know that almost all emeralds have flaws? We call them the *jardin,* or garden, because when you look into the stone it looks like a pattern of foliage.' He put a portfolio of sketches onto the table and flicked through them. 'This one, I suggest,' he said fussily, pointing to one sketch. 'In platinum, not gold, to suit your colouring, and with trillion diamonds on either side to point up the magnificent colour of the stone. It would suit your hand very well.'

Lauren looked at it and then at the stone. Guy had said nothing, but when she glanced up he was watching her with tawny, half-closed eyes, and she coloured and glanced back at the stone she'd chosen.

It was utterly beautiful; perhaps, she thought as Guy and the jeweller went into technicalities, it was a symbol. Nothing was ever perfect; if she could be satisfied with a flawed stone, surely she could settle for a flawed marriage? She loved Guy, and even if he didn't love her, he wanted her.

It might not be enough, but shielding her emotions to protect herself was a coward's way, and she had never been a coward. She'd fought for her life when she'd been ill; she'd relished the chance to prove herself in her career.

If she didn't fight for this man she'd never be able to look herself in the face again.

'Still sure that that's the one?' Guy asked. 'This one is flawless, if you'd prefer that.'

'No,' she said, shaking her head. 'The colour is breathtaking, and I like the idea of having my own garden on my finger.'

She met the quizzical gleam of his gaze with head high, relaxing only when he turned to the jeweller.

'In that case, we'll have it. Thank you.'

CHAPTER ELEVEN

THE choosing of the ring and the Press release signalled a month of intense—almost frenzied—activity.

The day before the ceremony, Lauren sank into a chair in the small parlour at the villa and slid her shoes from her aching feet.

'By now I must have met every person on the island who has the least interest in this marriage,' she told her mother drily. 'There were over five hundred people at the garden party, and they all wanted to tell me how much they liked Guy, and how lucky I am. Especially the women.'

Her mother nodded. 'He's also very popular with the men, which is so important, isn't it? Your father likes him very much.'

When Guy came strolling through with her father, Lauren leaned back and fixed him with a steely gaze. 'I seem to remember you saying once that apart from a sentimental affection for the island, you had little to do with it. Clearly the Dacians don't feel anything as mild as a sentimental affection for you—adulation describes it better.'

He grinned and put a long glass of fruit juice on the table beside her. 'I told you they loved weddings.'

'That's not it,' she said, grateful for the glossy, seamless façade she'd developed over the past hectic weeks. 'They love you. Someone told me today that you had given the government of Sant'Rosa the mobile-telephone network that connects the village chiefs.'

He shrugged. 'Good advertising,' he said calmly.

Her brows shot up. 'On Sant'Rosa? He said that you also fund an air ambulance that's already cut the death rate there.'

'Even better advertising.'

His bored tone effectively silenced her. Picking up the glass of juice, she sipped it while he spoke to her parents.

In this past hectic month she'd learned a lot about the man she loved—always from others. Guy himself had transmuted into a sophisticated stranger who wore power and position like an extension of himself. As they went about their duties she sensed beneath his consideration and courtesy an inner withdrawal that hurt her as much as her unrequited love.

In twenty-four hours he would be her husband, but she still had no idea whether he intended it to be a real marriage, or one in name only. Their public duties and her parents' constant presence meant that they hadn't had a chance to discuss anything beyond arrangements for the wedding.

He'd made no move to secure them some private moments.

He had only touched her when it was necessary, and although he'd kissed her hand—even lightly kissed her on occasion—it had been for the benefit of the family and close friends who'd gathered to celebrate.

The panic that had been building over the weeks clogged her throat; she sipped more juice, gratefully letting the tangy sweetness ease the blockage, but it did nothing for the deep, unfathomable sadness that coloured every waking moment.

As though he felt her tension, Guy said, 'Come for a walk in the garden.'

Surprised, she went with him out onto the terrace and down the shady length of the garden, saying nothing while her heart and mind and body sang with forbidden delight.

'Is everything all right?' he asked.

'Yes, of course.'

He stopped in the heavy shade of a tree and scrutinised her face. Lauren held his regard without flinching.

A hard smile curved his mouth. 'Arrogant,' he said, not without satisfaction. 'I like it when your eyes flash diamond fire at me. Your mother is worried about you.'

Feeling her way, she said, 'It's just a hangover from when I was ill. If I look a bit tired it's because I'm not used to playing princess.'

'You do it brilliantly.' But he didn't look convinced.

Standing her ground against his intense golden scrutiny, she admitted, 'I watch Alexa and follow her example.'

'And she learnt from my cousin Lucia,' he said, still watching her with hooded eyes.

Lauren nodded. She didn't know whether the beautiful Princess Lucia, Mrs Hunt Radcliffe, liked her or not; she suspected not. She even understood why. Sensible, intelligent women, both fond of Guy, Alexa and Lucia must sense that all was not normal in the relationship.

'What do we need to discuss?' she asked politely.

He put a hand in his pocket and pulled out a river of emerald fire. 'I want to give you this.' He dropped the necklace with its pendant stone over her head. 'I know that most brides wear pearls, but not royal brides in Dacia,' he said with a hard twist of his lips as he stepped back to examine the necklace on her. 'Emeralds are supposed to endow their wearers with the power to predict the future.'

'Very useful.' If only...

Her hand came up to touch the cool stone. 'I—thank you. I've got you something too, but it's not—'

'I don't need any more cuff-links,' he said laconically.

'So it's just as well I didn't buy you any,' she snapped.

Tension drummed between them, dark and heavy as the shade of the tree, eventually broken by Guy's rueful voice. 'I'm sorry, that was uncalled for. I know that whatever you give me will be as unusual—and as beautiful—as you are.'

The practised compliment grated. 'Unusual?' she asked with a lift of her brows.

'Didn't you know?' He leaned back against the trunk of the tree, the dappled shade that played across the aquiline features hiding any nuances of expression. 'On the outside you're the epitome of cool sophistication, yet you've won the hearts of these conservative islanders with your grace and your laughter and your interest in them. I suspect that glossy exterior is only a veneer.'

'No one reveals themselves openly to strangers,' she said uncertainly.

He was silent for a heartbeat, before saying tonelessly, 'Of course you're right.'

Summoning a smile, she touched the glowing green gems on her breast. 'Thank you for this. It's magnificent, and I'll wear it with pride in the tradition.' Her smile fading, she added steadily, 'And I believe it's also traditional to quarrel the day before the wedding.'

Laughing softly, he straightened. The sounds of the birds dwindled into nothingness; eyes widening, Lauren watched him come towards her, so big he blocked everything from her sight.

'So perhaps,' he said deliberately, 'we should end this very minor quarrel the traditional way.'

Excitement beat high within her and she lifted her face in instinctive invitation. With an odd, raw sound he caught her in his arms.

Her lashes fluttered down, but lifted within a few seconds when the kiss she expected didn't eventuate. He was looking at her with scorching intensity, tawny eyes narrowed and piercing.

Through lips that scarcely moved, he said, 'But I don't think this can be the traditional kiss of peace. There is nothing peaceful about the way I want you. It eats into my guts and steals my mind and shatters my sleep and shoots holes in my control. You are a torment to me.'

Lauren's lips trembled. Nothing about love, but it was enough—for the moment. Oh, she might regret this, but for now she needed him.

She reached up and pulled his head down and opened her mouth to him without dissembling or holding back.

Hunger, fire, need, the aching demand for completion, sharp and sweet and fiery, the longing for something more than this physical flash and glamour—and a potent glory in the taste and feel and scent of him—all combined to hurl her into waters that closed over her head.

It was Guy who pulled back, Guy who muttered something outrageous beneath his breath in three languages, one of which she knew, and Guy who said on a half-laugh that held both satisfaction and regret, 'Darling heart, someone is coming—several someones, in fact, talking loudly enough to warn us.'

Only then did Lauren hear the voices; crashing back to earth, she groaned.

'I so agree,' Guy said, irony glimmering in the depths of his eyes, and dropped a swift kiss on the tip of her nose before letting her go and running a hand through his hair—hair she'd disarranged with her fingers.

For a second she saw the man she'd fallen in love with on Sant'Rosa, but in the space of a breath he donned the mask again, replacing the buccaneer with the worldly prince and tycoon.

The intruders were her parents, followed by Marc and his wife, Paige, with their two children, twin girls of three, who'd arrived a few hours previously and were staying in another house owned by Prince Luka.

Introductions performed, Lauren gave in to the appeals of the two small girls and sank to her knees, hugging them to her. 'Darlings,' she said extravagantly, 'how are my two favourite girls in all the world?'

They babbled happily in a mixture of French and English, one in each ear as they pressed soft, moist kisses to her cheeks. Heart overflowing, she gathered both for another big hug. When she looked up it was to see Guy watching her, his expression totally devoid of expression. A cold chill of disappointment whispered through her, but she smiled and laughed and chattered for an hour until they left.

Marc managed a word with her. A small frown drawing his brows together, he said, 'Is everything all right?'

Deliberately misunderstanding him she bestowed her sunniest smile on him. 'Not you too! My mother has been watching me like a hawk, and I'm surprised Guy doesn't take my pulse every hour. I only had pneumonia, for heaven's sake, and I'm well over it now.'

His frown deepened. 'I know you too well. You look fragile.'

Aware that Guy was watching them, she said brightly, 'All brides totter up the aisle in an exhausted state—it's tradition! Your bone marrow is still doing excellent work.'

He didn't pursue it. 'If you ever need me,' he said in a voice she'd heard only a couple of times, 'contact me or Paige.'

'Thank you, but I won't need you,' she said, hoping her voice didn't sound as brittle as her emotions.

Later, after what Alexa had referred to somewhat wryly as, 'Just a family dinner for eighty people in the Little Palace,' Lauren watched Guy charm them all— the rich, the successful, the titled and the beautiful, she thought sardonically.

Her mother laughed at a witticism from an elderly Austrian duke, and her father obviously enjoyed the company of a younger woman whose face was so familiar she had to be famous.

'That's a somewhat *triste* expression,' Guy commented from behind.

She turned, bracing herself to meet his burnished eyes. At least the kiss had told her that behind his unreadable façade was the man who wanted her. She clung to that knowledge with passionate intensity, because it warmed her; inside she might be dying, but at least Guy desired her as much as she did him.

It would have to be enough.

'All right,' she said softly, 'I admit that I am just the tiniest bit tired. Everything's gone like a dream, and no one could have been nicer to me and my family than your cousins and the Dacians and everyone I've met, but I am really looking forward to all this being over.'

'This time tomorrow,' he promised, 'you'll be able to relax.'

They had decided to spend the first night in his house on Dacia; Guy had refused to take her there so that it would be a surprise. After that they'd fly to a small Caribbean island that belonged to a friend of his.

He took her hand, feeling it tremble in his, and fought back a pang of lust so potent it almost unmanned him then and there. He'd spent a wretched month grinding down the temptation to take her, and the kiss they'd exchanged that afternoon had been small solace. Whatever she felt for him, she had no control over this physical craving. Like him she was inextricably bound to it, barely able to control it, completely unable to overcome it.

Once the decision had been made she'd thrown herself into learning to do as good a job as Alexa and Lucia, succeeding brilliantly, but the shadows darkening her clear eyes worried him.

Something compelled him to say, 'Do you trust me, Lauren?'

She gave him a startled look that refused to engage with his eyes. 'Of course— I wouldn't be going through with this if I mistrusted you.'

Her words didn't satisfy him, but as he didn't know what answer he wanted this wasn't surprising. Perhaps he too was tired, he thought ironically, nodding as Luka glanced across the room.

'It's time to go,' he said. 'Sleep well tonight, my heart.'

A clouded glance and a tight smile were her only response, and he wondered what was going on in the sleek black head behind those deceptively translucent eyes. Other women had always been easy to read.

Lauren kept her thoughts and her emotions to herself; only in his arms could he tell what she was feeling, and even then, her mind was closed against him.

From his lovers he'd never asked anything more than companionship and the willing and enthusiastic sharing of their bodies, but with Lauren he faced the compulsion to storm her guarded heart.

CHAPTER TWELVE

For Lauren, the next day passed in a daze: thousands of Dacians cheering as the open coach passed through the streets, its white horses decked in a panoply of silver and white; the solemnity of the service, the flickering lights of candles and the glorious singing; the poignant moments when Guy slid her ring onto her finger and after she had done the same for him they were pronounced man and wife; the wild, jubilant clangour of the bells as they turned to face the congregation.

Together, they were pelted with flower petals on the short trip in an open carriage back to the Old Palace. They floated on the air, some settling like coloured snowflakes on the skirt of Lauren's gorgeous dress. The couturier, a small, determined despot in her mid-sixties, had searched the world for silk in exactly the right shade.

'With the faintest hint of pink,' she'd explained, contemptuously tossing discarded samples onto the bench. 'Otherwise with that white, white skin you will look like a marble statue, not a living, breathing bride for our prince!'

She had found what she wanted in India, and transformed it into a dress that took the breath away. Now, with a bouquet of moon-coloured roses on the seat beside the coachman, and the excited roar of the crowds in her ears, Lauren smiled until her cheeks ached, and then smiled some more, waving as she'd been taught.

They were almost at the Old Palace when she turned

to Guy and said, 'I see what you mean when you told me Dacians adore a good wedding! This is overwhelming.'

He laughed and looked down into her face with kindling eyes. 'They love you too,' he said. His voice deepened. 'Can you hear what they're calling? *Beautiful lady—*'

Dazzled, she caught a glitter of metal from the corner of her eye. Time froze—a silver blade splashed with scarlet flamed under the hot sun, aiming straight for Guy's chest.

People screamed as she tried to fling herself across him; he pushed her away, twisting his big body to shield her, and the object hit his shoulder before rolling harmlessly in the drifts of flower petals on the floor.

Grey-faced, he gave it one searing glance, then turned and said her name on a note of raw pain as he pulled her upright with exquisite tenderness.

Against a cry of people and the sharp clatter of the horses' hooves as the postilions fought to control them, she gasped, 'Are you hurt? God, are you hurt?'

'No. It's all right, it's not a bomb.' Locking her against him, he barked out an order to the security man who appeared from nowhere to scoop up the object, a roll of paper with an incongruous red rose tied on to it by silver ribbons.

'I'm fine,' she said against the cries of the crowd. 'It didn't even touch me. What is it?'

The crowd noise changed from panic to vengefulness, and Guy released her, setting her back on the seat, such cold fury hardening his face that she had to stop herself from shrinking back.

He called out another order, and the man who'd thrown the object was shoved unceremoniously towards them, some of the outraged people striking at him as he was pushed up to the carriage.

Only young, about eighteen, he looked terrified. Adrenaline pumping through her in devastating surges, Lauren listened without comprehension to the rapid-fire conversation that took place between Guy and the youth. When the crowd, so ugly a moment ago, began to laugh, she caught her breath.

Although Guy was frowning when he turned to her, the black anger had faded. 'It is a petition,' he said softly, grasping her cold hands. 'He wishes to apologise for frightening you—see, he tied a rose to it so that you would know it wasn't dangerous.'

Shock had set her teeth chattering, but she gritted them and said, 'Tell him that if he ever throws anything at you again—no, you'd better not. What should I say?'

'That you forgive him this time but suggest he uses more conventional methods to present a petition?' he suggested, and when she nodded he dropped a fleeting kiss on her hand and turned to the youth. Crisply he conveyed Lauren's words.

From behind the living barriers of soldiers people called out to Lauren. Straightening her spine, she saw concern and affection and lingering shock in their faces. One woman was weeping silently.

Still shaking, Lauren managed a smile and a wave, and the Dacians cheered and blew kisses, and cheered again as the youth was hurried off and the horses urged on their way.

Guy's hand closed around hers, warm and firm and reassuring. 'I could kill him, the fool,' he ground out.

She shivered, but maintained that smile. 'I thought— I feel an utter idiot. I thought it was a dagger or something like that.'

'You have fast reactions,' he said quietly. 'If it had been a dagger it could have killed you.'

If it had been a bomb it would have killed them both. At least, she thought, reaction leading to something perilously close to hysteria, they'd have died together.

'Thank God it wasn't,' she said devoutly. 'What on earth made him think of such a thing?'

Guy gave her an unreadable glance. 'He wishes to marry, but his mother doesn't want it,' he said gravely. 'He was sure we'd be able to talk her into a better frame of mind, so he chose this way to dramatise his situation. He thought we would understand from the rose that we shouldn't be afraid.'

Lauren stared at him, then said in a voice that trembled uncontrollably, 'If I start laughing now I'm going to end up with full-blown hysterics, so I'll save it for later.'

'A wise decision,' her husband agreed solemnly, and they waved and smiled to the cheering crowd. But Lauren's hand remained in Guy's until they reached the Old Palace.

Much later, after a banquet and farewells to her parents and Paige and Marc, they drove out from the palace as dusk was falling. Guy was behind the wheel, and soon they left the partying islanders behind for the narrow roads to the other side of Dacia.

Neither spoke for a long time, until Guy said, 'How do you feel?'

'Still a bit hyped,' she admitted. 'And I probably drank a glass too much of that delicious champagne. How about you?'

'I alternate between wanting to dismember the kid slowly, and being grateful that's all it was. Luka is furious; the security service will be going to bed with a flea in its collective ear.' He turned off the road onto a private one, and a few minutes later they stopped outside his house.

Her first glimpse startled her. 'I thought it would be old,' she exclaimed, tension thinning her tone into a travesty of her normal voice. Lights blazed all along the double-storeyed modern building, and a man was running out to meet the car.

'Are you disappointed?'

'No,' she said quietly, looking around her at the gracious lines and ambience of the building. 'This is beautiful, and it suits you.'

Inside it was spacious and airy, the scent of the sea mingling with those from the gardens. Someone had gone crazy with roses—not the red blooms of passion, but old-fashioned flowers in milky colours, their scent overpowering on the warm, dry air.

And candles—tall white candles bloomed with golden tips amidst the flowers.

'This is so beautiful,' Lauren breathed, looking around her with astonishment. She glanced up at Guy's angular face, then away again. 'Will you thank whoever thought of it and the ones who did it?'

'I will.' He introduced a housekeeper and two maids, conveying her thanks in rapid Dacian.

They beamed at her, and then the housekeeper showed her to a huge bedroom, indicating a sumptuous bathroom and the wide glass doors that opened out onto a tiled terrace. More flowers hazed the room with perfume, more candles glowed softly on the dresser, and she saw with a pang that the bed had been covered with rose petals in the same shades of white and dusky pink and subtle, old-fashioned reds.

Her clothes had been delivered that morning; no

doubt Guy's had been too, but they weren't hanging with hers in the room-sized wardrobe.

So she would be the only one to sleep in that beautiful bed. Guy probably planned to make love with her there, but afterwards he would go back to his own room.

Gripped by acute, devastating disappointment, she walked out onto the terrace and stood for a long, lonely time while the stars bloomed above her and waves purred onto a white beach not far below. A faint whisper of sound, soft as satin, came from a fountain somewhere, and the air was fragrant and silky on her bare arms.

Eventually she set her jaw and went back inside to change from her exquisite going-away outfit in pale silk to something more suitable for an evening with the husband who didn't want anything more from her than the temporary use of her body.

If he wanted that. The empty wardrobe indicated that he didn't plan to share his life with her.

Guy showed her around the austerely beautiful house, showed her how the security system worked, and then said, 'You look exhausted. The garden can wait for tomorrow. Why don't you have an early night?'

'Yes, I'll do that,' she said evenly, pain slicing through her.

Half an hour later, ready for bed in a pair of sleeveless cotton pyjamas, she looked at the enormous bed with its counterpane of petals, and shivered.

A knock on the door to the terrace whirled her around, and joy possessed her in a white-hot sunburst when she saw Guy there, only to fade when she realised he was still wearing the casually tailored trousers and fine cotton shirt he'd changed into after they'd got there.

She had to clear her throat to say, 'Come in.'

One step into the room made it his own; he dominated it with bold, unleashed power. Her heart began to beat faster.

Eyes narrowing, he said harshly, 'You've been bruised.'

'It's nothing,' she returned quickly, because his fingers had done the damage when he'd flung her out of the way of the missile.

But he came across and lightly touched the purpling blotches. 'I'm sorry—I wanted to get you out of the way. I thought it might have been a bomb. Have you anything to put on them?'

'They've already been anointed with arnica.' Her voice sounded distant, robbed of colour and texture.

He bent his head and kissed each bruise, his mouth lingering and tender. Little rills of sensation purled through her, sweet as love, sensuous as rapture...

Guy let her go, his face set in the distant expression she'd come to know so well during the past month. 'We have to talk.'

'I—all right.'

But he walked across to the open doors and with his back to her said, 'When I came to New Zealand, I told myself that it was to visit Lucia and Hunt—they live not far from the Bay of Islands—but I wanted to see how you fitted into Corbett's world.'

Something clicked into place. 'Did Lucia tell you I was Marc's mistress?'

'No. I'd already been told by a cousin.' He paused, then finished deliberately, 'Before I met you.'

So he'd known who she was when she'd turned up on Sant'Rosa.

He resumed, 'Lucia said there was a link between you and Corbett, but she didn't know what it was.

Everything seemed to back it up—you were staying in his house, you were terrified that the media would find out about our marriage...'

She angled her chin at him. 'Even if I had been his lover, what business would it have been of yours?'

'You can say that after the time we spent together in Valanu?'

'Oh, the sex was wonderful,' she agreed bleakly. 'But we made no commitment to each other.'

He swung around and directed a shaft of searing gold fire at her. 'I wanted you the second I saw you. When it seemed you were his mistress I despised myself for not being able to chisel that hunger from my body—but I knew right from the start that I wasn't going to give you up.'

Lauren breathed in sharply. 'But why—when you found out I wasn't Marc's lover, when you understood the reason I was so afraid of the media—why did you pull away? The minute we decided to marry again on Dacia you got colder and colder and harder and harder and more and more distant.'

'Because by then,' he said deliberately, 'and without acknowledging it, not even to myself—*especially* not to myself—I was head over heels in love with you. And you were not in love with me. You made it obvious—frequently!—that the last thing you wanted was the marriage I'd forced on you.'

Lauren's pulses jumped, but she shook her head in disbelief. 'You might have railroaded me, but I was the one who gained. That first marriage saved me from—at the least—a nasty experience in a very unsavoury gaol. And the second time you offered—insisted!—on formalising our marriage, partly it was to protect me and my family if our private lives and sins were hung out to dry.'

His mouth curved sardonically. 'That was partly the truth. Just as the way the Dacians feel is part of the truth. But only part. When I came back from the States I saw that you hadn't been sleeping, and I knew then that I had to offer you your freedom because I couldn't bear to chain you to me. And that's when I knew I loved you.'

Too shocked to be able to believe him, she breathed, 'And I turned you down.'

'Yes, you were very stiff about keeping your promises. I started to hope then.'

'But you didn't—'

'Didn't woo you?' he said when she fell silent. 'When did we have the opportunity? The decision had to be yours—it is still yours. If you ask me to go back to my room, I will do that.' His grin briefly illuminated his face. 'Of course, I won't promise to stop trying to make you fall in love with me.'

'For a man of your experience,' she said, so quietly she could barely hear her words above the singing of her heart, 'you've been awfully obtuse. Of course I love you. Not that I admitted it—I kept trying to convince myself that I was just like my mother, I'd jumped head-long into a sizzling infatuation—but I wouldn't have made love with you on Valanu if I hadn't loved you. But when I arrived here and found out who you were, I knew that it had just been a dream of love, a fantasy.'

'Why?' he demanded. And when she didn't answer he said, 'Surely not because of your family history? That won't wash, Lauren. It's not as though anyone else cares—everyone knows about Alexa's father.'

'Her grandfather was a prince,' she said quietly.

He gave a hard laugh. 'All right, if it's bloodlines you're concerned about— Hunt, Lucia's husband, fought his way up from a foster home with nothing but his guts and intelligence and determination.'

'Yes,' she said simply, 'but he's rich.'

'Lucia didn't marry him for his money.'

She wanted him to convince her with his kisses, with his love, but he stayed three paces distant. 'I know, but there's no scandal in his past, only poverty. And you know perfectly well that old scandals cast long shadows.'

'Lauren, it doesn't matter. It will never matter. You have courage and a brain as well as a warm heart and a charm that has everyone on their knees in minutes— from little Nico to Luka, who is a much tougher nut than his son.' With an exasperated shake of his head he finished, 'I would never have thought you lacked self-esteem!'

Lauren looked at him, saw the truth naked in his eyes and his face, and a huge weight she hadn't been conscious of rolled away, leaving her so light and carefree she almost laughed with the joy of it.

Speaking carefully, groping for her own particular truth, she said, 'I think I convinced myself that my past was utterly shameful partly because I didn't want people to sneer at my mother, but also because it kept me safe. Love had to be terrifying if my mother could almost throw away a good marriage.' She hesitated before continuing, 'But it wasn't like that. My birth father met her at a particularly vulnerable time in her life, when she'd just discovered that she wasn't likely to ever have children. She said she felt like a failure as a woman. He was kind, he made her feel feminine and desired. But she soon came to her senses—only to find that she was pregnant with his child.'

'Does that hurt you?'

'No. My *real* father— Hugh—has never stopped loving her, and she loves him too. I'm not perfect, so why should I expect my mother to be?'

'I'm not perfect either,' Guy said. He paused, and she heard the fountain outside whispering softly in the darkness.

He said deeply, 'But I will love you until the day I die, and I will never be unfaithful to you.'

Tears ached behind her eyes. 'I love you. I might kill you if you even think of being unfaithful to me, but I will be true to you, I promise.'

He flung his head back and laughed, the angry tension of the past weeks dissolving like sugar in the mouth, so that he was free and younger than he had ever been. 'Killing me would certainly put a stop to any unfaithfulness,' he agreed. He sobered quickly, and said, 'But it is not something you will ever need to contemplate. I mean what I say. You are all that I want.' He looked more closely at her, and said in a shaken voice, 'Tears, my heart?'

She blinked them back; they could not be allowed to sully this precious moment. 'These past weeks have been hideous. I felt as though I was living two lives, and both of them were false. I could feel you pulling away and I didn't know what to do about it because you said you didn't want to marry me—'

'Only after you'd said flatly that you hated this whole business,' he cut in. 'I wanted you to feel safe—to know that I wouldn't force myself on you once we were married—although I had every intention of seducing you!'

Lauren gave him a glimmering smile. 'Idiots, both of

us. Utter and complete idiots. I'm surprised you didn't understand what was happening to me—after all, I'm not your first lover. And I've seen your effect on women. You catch everyone's eyes just by walking into the room!'

He ignored the faint note of bitterness. 'But you're the only woman I've ever loved,' he said, and at last he reached out for her and they came together and exchanged their first kiss without barriers.

'And the only woman I will ever love. It's so different,' he said quietly, stroking her hair back from her face. 'Loving you makes me vulnerable and at first I hated that. Then I kept remembering you as you were on Valanu, warm and loving and passionate, and despising myself because something I'd done had changed you.'

'Falling in love has that effect on people,' she said into his neck.

He glanced down at her pyjamas. 'I forbid you ever to wear anything like this again,' he said sternly. 'You look far too young and sweet in them. From now on you must wear silk when you come to bed with me.'

Suddenly radiant, Lauren laughed. 'Everyone has been telling me that a good marriage involves compromise, so because I love you I'll wear silk, but you have to make a concession too.'

'Certainly.'

She kissed the fine-grained skin of his shoulder, relishing the way the muscle hardened and flexed beneath her questing lips. 'No clothes,' she said succinctly, and ran her hand down to the waist of his trousers, pushing them down.

Laughing, Guy let her strip him, and then he did the same for her before carrying her across to the bed, where the laughter faded into passion and at last they made love with no defences, no inhibitions, nothing to spoil the complete union both had longed for.

Eventually, when she was lying against him, listening to the solid drumming of his heart as it eased into a normal beat, she said, 'I thought you were going to leave me alone tonight.'

His chest lifted. 'I'd planned to, but when that young idiot hurled his ridiculous petition, you tried to fling yourself in front of me.' Stone faced, he looked at her. 'The only thing that stopped me from killing him without mercy there and then was that it seemed to mean you had some feelings for me.'

'I see,' she said shakily.

'It gave me hope.' He rolled her on top of him and in the darkness she caught the white flash of his smile. 'The pretty wedding Alexa put on for us wasn't necessary, but I have to admit that I am glad. Once in his life, every man should feel as I did when you walked down the aisle towards me in that exquisite dress, with my ring on your finger and flowers in your arms. Until then I felt that perhaps I could let you go if you wanted to leave after a couple of years. But when I saw you then, I knew that I would do anything to make you love me.'

Unbearably moved, she dropped a kiss on the point of his chin. 'You could have told me,' she said indignantly. 'You must have known how I felt about you!'

'I didn't want to use the sexual charge between us to dazzle you into thinking you loved me,' he said, a sombre note intensifying his meaning. 'I need more than the unwilling response of your body, no matter how magnificent that is for us both.'

She shivered, because magnificent described exactly

how she felt when they made love—as though the world and everything in it had been made for them.

'You hid it well,' she complained, but with a note of understanding in her voice.

'So did you,' he returned. 'Shall we make a vow never to hide big things from each other again? I don't want to bore you with details of business—'

'Now that, I'd find very interesting!'

'So that was a poor example,' he said, laughing softly. 'But if you are sad I want to know why, and if you are happy I want to share your happiness.'

'And the same applies to you. No shutting me out again. I thought I'd wither away.'

He kissed her softly, and then not quite so softly, and then said, 'We must find work for you to do—you are not going to be happy organising charity events.'

'No,' she said instantly. 'Where are we going to live?'

'Wherever you want to.' When she didn't answer he said, 'Paris, if that would please you.'

'I'd love to live there,' she told him, 'but my parents are already in love with Dacia. Yesterday Dad said something about buying a house here. Would it be too inconvenient if we lived here too?'

'They won't be able to buy a house. Dacian property belongs to Dacians, but they can rent. And I'd be very happy to stay on the island; when our children come along it will be good for them to have their only set of grandparents living close by, and to play with the island children as I did, and with Luka and Alexa's brood. I think it will be good for your father's health, also.'

She kissed him and after a long, passionate interlude, confessed, 'When we make love, I feel as though I might die of pleasure.'

Guy laughed softly. 'No one ever died of pleasure, my sweet one.'

Snuggling against him, she murmured, 'And if I did, one kiss from you would bring me back to life.' She jackknifed upright. 'Your present!'

Golden eyes gleaming, he said deeply, 'I have already had it.'

She laughed and groped under the pillow. 'Your *wedding* present,' she said, hauling out a small jeweller's box.

He looked at it in surprise. Long tanned fingers flicked it open, and he saw the ring she'd had made for him, a signet ring with the leopard of Dacia carved into the face. Jauntily, wickedly, a tiny emerald eye glittered in the heraldic beast's head.

Suddenly uncertain, Lauren watched as he slid it onto his finger. 'I know your other one is precious to you,' she began.

'Doubly precious because you wore it. This is more precious because you gave it to me,' he said.

He laughed, rich and deep and satisfied, and pulled her down beside him. 'Lauren, I love you,' he said on a raw note. 'With all my heart, with everything I have, everything I am, more and more each day. I will love you until I die.'

Joy expanded to fill her completely. From now on, she thought happily as she drifted off to sleep in his arms, and no matter what happened, they would be safe together, she and her prince.

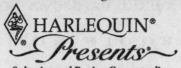

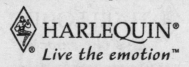

Receive a FREE hardcover book from

HARLEQUIN ROMANCE®

in September!

Harlequin Romance celebrates the launch of the line's new cover design by offering you this exclusive offer valid only in September, only in Harlequin Romance.

To receive your FREE HARDCOVER BOOK written by bestselling author Emilie Richards, send us four proofs of purchase from any September 2004 Harlequin Romance books. Further details and proofs of purchase can be found in all September 2004 Harlequin Romance books.

Must be postmarked no later than October 31.

Don't forget to be one of the first to pick up a copy of the new-look Harlequin Romance novels in September!

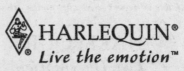

Visit us at www.eHarlequin.com

HRPOP0904

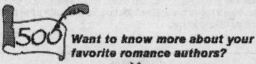

If you enjoyed what you just read,
then we've got an offer you can't resist!

Take 2 bestselling
love stories FREE!
Plus get a FREE surprise gift!

The world's bestselling romance series.

HARLEQUIN®
Presents

Seduction and Passion Guaranteed!

THEPRINCESSBRIDES

For duty, for money…for passion!

Discover a thrilling new trilogy from a rising star of Harlequin
Presents®, Jane Porter!

Meet the Royals…

Chantal, Nicolette and Joelle are members of the blue-blooded
Ducasse family. Step inside their sophisticated and glamorous
world and watch as these beautiful princesses find they have
to marry three international playboys—for duty, for money…
and definitely for passion!

Don't miss

THE SULTAN'S BOUGHT BRIDE (#2418)
September 2004

THE GREEK'S ROYAL MISTRESS (#2424)
October 2004

THE ITALIAN'S VIRGIN PRINCESS (#2430)
November 2004

**Pick up a Harlequin Presents® novel and you will enter a world
of spine-tingling passion and provocative, tantalizing romance!**

Available wherever Harlequin books are sold.

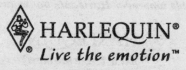

HARLEQUIN®
Live the emotion™

www.eHarlequin.com

HPPBJPOR

The world's bestselling romance series.

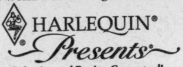

HARLEQUIN®
Presents~

Seduction and Passion Guaranteed!

Legally wed,
Great together in bed,
But he's never said…
"I love you"

They're…

Wedlocked!

The series
where marriages
are made in
haste…and love
comes later….

Don't miss
HIS CONVENIENT MARRIAGE by Sara Craven #2417
on sale September 2004

Coming soon
MISTRESS TO HER HUSBAND by Penny Jordan #2421
on sale October 2004

**Pick up a Harlequin Presents® novel and you will
enter a world of spine-tingling passion and
provocative, tantalizing romance!**

Available wherever Harlequin books are sold.

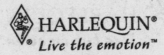

HARLEQUIN®
Live the emotion™

www.eHarlequin.com   HPWEDSO